Spirits, Rock Stars, and a Midnight Chocolate Bar

Pyper Rayne Series, Book 2

by
Deanna Chase

Copyright © 2016 by Deanna Chase
First Edition 2016
ISBN 978-1-940299-39-6

Cover Art by Janet Holmes
Editing by Anne Victory and Angie Ramey

This book is a work of fiction. Names, characters, places, and incidents are products of the author's imagination or are used fictitiously. Any resemblance to actual events, locals, business establishments, or persons, living or dead, are entirely coincidental.

Bayou Moon Publishing

About This Book

It's date night! And medium Pyper Rayne is finally getting some alone time with her oh-so-sexy new boyfriend, Julius. But when a representative from the Witches' Council shows up during appetizers, the romance portion of the evening comes to a screeching halt. Julius is needed to deal with paranormal activity—on a cruise ship to the Caribbean.

An all-expense paid cruise to the Caribbean sounds like the perfect second date… until Pyper witnesses the death of a famous rock star. Suddenly Pyper and Julius are caught in the middle of a decade-old homicide. Now the race is on to solve the mystery or history is destined to repeat itself.

Chapter 1

THE BELL ON the door chimed, and I glanced up from my table, smiling. Julius, my date, strolled into the Grind—the café I owned—looking every bit the 1920s gangster: black pants, black dress shirt, black-and-white pin-striped vest, and a white silk tie. To top it all off, he'd even added a fedora. Butterflies did a swan dive in my stomach. God, he was sexy.

"Hot damn!" Ida May, my resident ghost, fanned herself while floating in the middle of my café. "If I were you, I'd forget the restaurant. Just haul his fine ass right upstairs, smother him in gravy, and eat him for dinner."

Now that was a thought. I grinned at her. Not long after I'd acquired my medium ability, Ida May had shown up and never left. At least she kept things interesting.

Holding a bouquet of blue violets, Julius ignored the circle of female tourists gaping at him and walked toward me. He was unlike anyone I'd ever dated before. The fact that he'd been a ghost for ninety or so years prior to being brought back to his human form probably had something to do with that. His gentlemanly manners charmed me while his secret, back-alley bootlegging persona did things to my girly parts. Skirting the law had been his way of surviving in the early nineteen hundreds in New Orleans.

"Hey there, handsome," I said as an unfamiliar ball of warmth sprang to life in my chest, a ball that felt suspiciously like… happiness. An alarm bell rang somewhere in the back of my mind, warning me to be careful. To keep my guard up, to not get burned yet again. But I instantly slammed the door on those thoughts.

Today I was going to enjoy myself… enjoy Julius.

Julius stopped midstep and frowned. "What's wrong?" He glanced down at his attire. "Too dated? Too old-fashioned?" Smiling, he added, "Is my fly down?"

"Not yet," Ida May said in a singsong voice. "But I'm sure Pyper would *love* to help you out with that."

Julius's cheeks flooded with color as he flushed with embarrassment. He was a witch who also had the gift of seeing spirits… much to his dismay when Ida May was around.

My heart nearly melted and I shook my head, chuckling. "No, you look very handsome. Very New Orleans."

"Very lickable." Ida May smacked her lips and ran her fingertips over the swell of her breast as if imagining what it would be like to do exactly that.

I eyed the 1920s ghost hovering beside me. She wore a lacy, sleeveless nightgown and black thigh-highs, a fitting outfit for someone who'd been one of the ladies of Storyville—the former New Orleans red-light district. "Ida May, I know you're the expert, but I'm pretty sure we can manage without your input."

"Damn straight I am. Did you know the quickest way to make a guy orgasm is to—"

"Ida May!" I laughed. "Stop."

"Wait, I might want to hear this." Julius slipped his arm

around my waist and pulled me closer to him, waiting for Ida May's answer.

I raised one skeptical eyebrow. "Is speed really the goal?"

He cleared his throat. "Perhaps not." Then he winked at me and tugged me toward the front door. "Let's hurry and get dinner so we can savor what comes next."

"Please." Ida May smirked. "You two are wound so tight, I bet you finish each other off before you even get naked."

Julius stared at her with his mouth slightly open.

I tightened my hand around his and shook my head in amusement. "Ignore her," I whispered to him. "She's just spun up because she hasn't seen any action in over ninety years."

"I heard that!" Ida May yelled as we slipped out the door.

"Where to?" I asked, tightening my short trench coat against the February chill, though my skirt and knee-high boots did nothing to warm my bare thighs.

"Dinner." He slipped his hand to the small of my back and led me down Bourbon Street, away from the crowds. "How does steak and those truffle fries you've been talking about sound?"

I licked my lips and suppressed a moan. "Truffle fries. You're angling for date of the year, aren't you?"

His eyes began to smolder as he swept his gaze over me. "If I'm lucky."

I leaned into him, lightly pressing my body to his long, firm one. "Oh, you're going to get lucky. No doubt about it."

It was his turn to suppress a groan. Quickening his pace, he tugged me along. "I hope you already know what you want to order, because dinner is going to be a quick affair."

A tingle of anticipation flitted through me, and I lengthened my stride to keep up with him. Before I knew it, we'd arrived at the restaurant and were being seated near the window. The scent of roasting beef filled the air, making my stomach growl.

"Two glasses of the house cabernet," Julius said to the waitress.

With a nod, she hurried off. I smiled at my date and had no sooner shrugged out of my coat than I felt the brush of ice-cold air against my bare arm. A shimmering light appeared out of nowhere, and then a small 'pop' sounded as a thin, black-haired woman materialized in the chair next to me.

"Whoa!" I jumped up, holding my hands out. "Who the hell are you?"

"Lizette?" Julius frowned, his brows drawn together in confusion. "What are you doing here?"

"You know her?" I asked, eyeing the woman. She wore a shapeless black silk dress and an armful of silver bangles. She was elegant in a boho-chic way.

Julius turned his apologetic gaze on me. "Lizette is a council witch. She oversees any cases assigned to me."

"I see." I lowered myself back into my chair and glanced around, noting that no one seemed to pay any attention to the witch's sudden appearance. No doubt she'd used some sort of spell to minimize her disturbance.

"Lizette?" Julius leaned in, piercing her with his gaze. "I probably don't have to tell you you're ruining my date."

"That can't be helped," Lizette said, a whimsical lilt to her voice. She slid an unmarked envelope toward him. "We've got a situation, and you're the only witch currently unassigned. We need you to take this case, and timing is of the essence."

"But we're on a date," I interjected before Julius could

answer. "Don't you think you're overstepping just a bit?"

Julius slipped his hand over mine and squeezed gently, but when he spoke, it was to Lizette. "It can't wait, can it?"

The witch shook her head. "I'm afraid not. There's been a measurable disturbance of black magic on the *Illusion*. They've had complaints of sinister activity on the main deck: apparitions, stolen energy, possessions, et cetera. You've been booked on tonight's passage. They're holding the ship for you. It's a seven-day cruise. Pack accordingly."

"The ship?" Julius's eyes widened. "Where am I headed?"

"Wait just a minute," I said, making no effort to keep the irritation out of my tone. "You're sending him on a cruise? Now?" This wasn't happening. Julius just took the job with the Witches' Council. They couldn't seriously be sending him out to sea. Could they? Not when we were supposed to be spending our first night together.

Lizette let out an exaggerated sigh as she stood. "My apologies for interrupting you, but we were out of options. If a witch—or worse—is aboard the *Illusion* and playing with black magic, then lives are on the line." Then she stopped and stared at us, shaking her head. "Honestly, I can't believe you two are so upset about an all-expenses-paid trip to the Caribbean for the week. Most witches would be thanking me right now, not complaining."

"Two?" I asked, my outrage fleeing at the thought of some beach time in Jamaica.

"Yes, two," she barked. "For goddess's sake. Isn't that what I just said?"

Julius grinned at me and then sobered as he turned to Lizette. "My apologies. I daresay you took us by surprise. Do you have any more information? Has anyone been hurt?”

“So far we only have a handful of frightened folk and one who ran into a doorknob, trying to escape an apparition. But a small fire did break out in one of the staterooms, and it’s unclear if it was an accident or our perpetrator. The guest doesn’t seem to remember any details. You’ll need to use your skills to flush the black-magic user out before anything worse happens.”

“Understood.” Julius got to his feet and held his hand out to Lizette. “I’ll report back a week from today.”

“I expect e-mails daily.” Then, without even glancing at his outstretched hand, she snapped her fingers and disappeared into thin air.

✧ ✧ ✧

I HAD MY iPhone on speaker as I hastily threw a variety of clothing into my suitcase. “Do you think I should take my lace-up boots?” I asked Jade, whom I’d called as soon as we got back to my apartment.

“I don’t know. I’ve never been on a cruise. I guess if they fit in your bag, why not?” A door slammed on the other end of the line and her tone turned hushed as she asked, “But never mind that. What’s this about black magic? You know how dangerous that is. How could you agree to this?”

“Julius has to go. It’s his job.”

“But you don’t,” she insisted. “Pyper—”

“Forget it. So far no one has been harmed, and I’ll be with Julius the entire time. There’s no way I’m turning down a cruise to the Caribbean. I’ll call you when we get back. Give my love to Kane.”

And before she could answer, I disconnected.

Julius leaned against the doorframe of my bedroom, watching me, his expression unreadable.

"Almost ready," I said and threw in a sexy little black dress along with another pair of shoes.

"You don't have to go, you know."

I froze and then slowly straightened as I met his hooded gaze, disappointed that our time together was vanishing once again. It wasn't that I resented his job, it was that I was eager to finally sink into the relationship we'd barely started. "Does that mean you don't want me to?"

He shook his head. "No, that's not it at all, but it could be dangerous. The last thing I want to do is put you in the path of a dark witch."

I let out a small bark of laughter but sobered instantly at his frown. "Sorry. It's just that the past two years with Jade and Kane have been crisis after crisis. Not to mention the dirty cop who kidnapped Nissa and me a few weeks ago. But we showed him, didn't we? Girl power rules!" I pumped my fist and winked.

Amusement lit his dark eyes and he grinned. "You sure did."

"I'm fine if you're fine. Like I told Jade, no one has been hurt, and you'll be there to protect me. While you're working, I'll just be at the pool. Preferably at the swim-up bar. Sound good?"

"Sounds perfect to me." He eyed my suitcase. "Especially if you're planning on wearing that tiny black two-piece."

"Oh, I'm planning on wearing it." I lowered my voice, switching to a husky tone. "And letting you strip it off me."

Lust flickered in his gaze, and he swallowed hard. "Let's

hope I close this case tonight then, because I have plans. Detailed ones that require plenty of time."

"Plans? Oh." I fanned myself and threw my favorite short skirt in the bag.

"Many, many plans," he said and then disappeared into the other room to wait for me.

Five minutes later, I had my suitcase stuffed and my passport in hand. "I'm ready."

"I've never seen a woman pack so fast," he said as he held the door open for me.

"I have," Ida May chimed in from out of nowhere. "You can't imagine how fast a girl can get her stuff together when the law is after her. Of course, when the majority of her wardrobe is lingerie, it's not that hard to pack."

I narrowed my eyes at the ghost floating in the middle of the stairwell. "What are you doing here?"

"Going with you, of course." A huge grin spread across her face. "I can't wait to find a hot bachelor to haunt."

"Ida—"

"Relax." She rolled her eyes. "You won't even know I'm there."

Julius and I glanced at each other. There was a heavy dose of skepticism in his gaze.

I closed my eyes and sighed. "I'm not sure I could stop her even if I tried."

Julius shook his head. "Not likely."

"Damn straight," Ida May said, tossing her dark hair over her shoulder. "Now let's go. There's a pink-tini with my name on it."

Chapter 2

MUSIC BLARED THROUGH the invisible speakers in the cheeky ship bar called the Green Parrot. Decorated with porcelain parrots, plastic palm trees, and replica pirate-ship paraphernalia, the place was too shiny and plastic to instill much confidence in the drink quality. Not to mention all the glasses had skulls and crossbones on them and the specialty drink was called Smuggler's Southern Sangria. It was served in a thirty-two-ounce mason jar and looked like a hangover waiting to happen.

I'd opted for my old standby instead, relieved they had a fair variety of beers on tap. The bartender placed a mug of Turbodog in front of me and then turned her attention to another passenger.

Beer? Ida May wrinkled her nose. She was sitting on top of the bar just to my right, eyeing the dance floor. *Why didn't you get the pink-tini I asked for?*

"Unbelievable," I muttered out of the side of my mouth. "Maybe because you're a ghost. I'm not buying you a nine-dollar cocktail you can't even drink."

Cheapskate. She cast me an irritated glare and then floated over to the dance floor where she inserted herself between a gorgeous couple, swaying to Chris De Burgh's *The Lady in Red.* The woman stiffened, then shivered slightly, no doubt from Ida May's presence. Ida May paid no attention to her and proceeded to press her see-through form up against the tall man.

He frowned and pulled his girl toward him, holding her close. Ida May seemed oblivious, but after a moment, the couple retreated from the floor and huddled together as if the temperature had dropped twenty degrees.

Ida May scowled at them but quickly turned her sights on one incredibly good-looking waiter who was serving a table full of giggling, middle-aged women.

I shook my head and took a long sip of my beer. The ship had taken off just a few minutes after we'd arrived, and after dropping off our bags, Julius had gone straight to the stateroom in question to test it for any paranormal activity. I'd been left behind, stuck listening to Ida May talk about the romance she was going to have on the high seas.

It'd only taken five minutes of that torture before I'd decided a drink was in order and headed for the nearest bar. Perhaps I should've ordered something stronger, but since our dinner had been so rudely interrupted, I hadn't eaten yet and didn't want to be a drunken mess when I met up with Julius later.

"Hello there, stranger," a familiar voice said from behind me.

I twisted around so fast I nearly fell off the stool when I spotted the slender strawberry blonde. "Jade? What are you doing here?"

"Taking a last-minute cruise with my wonderful husband." She gestured behind her at Kane, my best friend, who stood talking to one of the ship stewards.

"I thought you were going to oversee the café?" I asked, already reaching for my phone, praying for a signal.

"Relax." She covered my hand with hers. "Charlie's got it covered. I know you're nervous about both of us being out of pocket for an entire week, but she knows what to do."

I tightened my hold around my phone, still tense, but let out a long, slow breath. The café was my baby. The thing I'd built that was all mine. It was hard to not worry, even though I knew it was in good hands. "You're right. I'm sure everything will be fine." Narrowing my eyes at her, I cocked my head to the side. "How did you two get last-minute tickets? Marc?"

Marc, her stepfather, was a council witch, but he was living in Idaho with her mother. If he was assigned to this case, things were way worse than we'd been led to believe.

"Oh, no. Kane called Maximus, who pulled some strings just in case there's any demon activity." She smiled as if her statement was totally normal. But then, in our world it *was* normal.

"Alrighty then." I waved the bartender down. "This lady needs a large drink. Bring her a margarita."

"Make it an iced tea for now," Jade said.

He nodded and got to work.

"Seriously?" I said. "You're gonna be sorry when I pass tipsy and head straight to foolville without you."

She laughed and hopped up on the stool. "Maybe. But I'm just happy to be here… Let vacation begin!"

"You? Vacation when magical forces are at play?" I laughed. "Right."

She pushed her hair back and shook her head. "Nope. This one's in Kane's and Julius's hands. I'm only here for the sunshine and beaches. And maybe a cheesy nightclub show or two."

"Did someone over here order an iced tea?" the bartender asked, holding a glass garnished with about a pound of tropical fruit.

"Right here." Jade grinned and slipped him a tip. "Thanks. This looks amazing."

"You let me know when you need a spiked version, all right?" he said with a wink.

Jade moaned her pleasure as she bit into a piece of mango.

I shook my head, focusing on the cutie behind the bar. "Maybe it's better if we just let her enjoy the moment."

"Gotcha." He winked at me and pocketed the bill. "I'll be here when you need me."

I need him right now, Ida May said with a fake growl. *Good gracious. So many hot men all in one place. I think I'm about to combust. Just five minutes, that's all I need. Five minutes until—*

"Time to go." I jumped up, ignoring her. When you're the only person in the room who can hear the ghost, it's best not speak lest you sound like a complete loon. "Jade, grab your drink. We're going on a midnight stroll."

It's not even eight o'clock yet! Ida May called as we walked out.

I glanced back just in time to see her grope the nearest man. He let out a startled yelp and hurried away, spilling his beer as he went.

"For the love of… Can't take that ghost anywhere," I said.

Jade snickered. "Ida May is here?"

Even though Jade was a witch, she couldn't see ghosts… usually. That was my special gift. And Julius's. Because he'd been one, he could usually see them when they were around.

"Yes. She tagged along, and short of exorcising her, there's nothing I can do about it. But Lord help me, if she interrupts my private time with Julius, she's on the first ghost train out of my life."

"Looks like she has plenty to keep her occupied." Jade led the way to the elevator. "I hear there's an adult-only pool and it's heated. Let's get our suits and have some fun."

✧　✧　✧

"IT'S COLDER THAN an ice queen's ass out here," I said, shivering at the side of the pool.

Jade gave me an impatient look as she treaded water. "Stop whining and get in. It's heated."

I glanced around, noting no one else was as crazy as we were. It was February, and we were headed into the Gulf of Mexico. While it wasn't exactly Alaska weather, there was still quite the windchill coming off the water. Reluctantly, I chucked my robe and hurried into the pool.

"Oh, gods," I said, sighing in pleasure as the warm water chased away the cold. "It's like a hot tub."

"Told you." She swam over to the edge of the pool where we'd left our drinks. "I know it's not the night either of us were exactly hoping for, but I think we recovered admirably."

"And what did you have on your agenda?" I asked as she handed me my beer.

She gave me a shy grin. "Baby-making. We've been actively trying since Chessandra was dethroned from the high-angel position and that nasty curse she put on me was broken. Now that our contract with her is void, we're concentrating on making a family."

I'd known they were thinking about trying to get pregnant, but things had been put on hold when Chessandra, the ruler of the angel realm had made the mistake of cursing Jade and Kane's future child. But once she was caught and the spell broken, she'd been fired and incarcerated. My eyes stung with happy tears as I gazed at my friend, my heart already swelling at the thought. "Seriously? You've finally decided to go for it? We're going to have a little witch or incubus running around soon?"

A quiet smile blossomed on her lips and her eyes shone with hope. "If we're lucky."

I put my beer down and wrapped my arms around her just as a soft melody from an acoustic guitar filled the air. The sound was moving, almost haunting in the darkness. And utterly gorgeous.

It seemed fitting she'd get serenaded after an announcement like that. Jade's family life hadn't been tragic by any means, but it hadn't been all chocolates and roses either. Hell, whose had? But both she and Kane had been abandoned one way or another while growing up, so starting a family was huge for them.

"A toast." I held my beer up and clinked it against her margarita glass. "To a little Rouquette baby and his or her most inappropriate aunt. I can't wait to corrupt the little bundle of joy."

Jade laughed. "Don't get too carried away. We need to make one first."

"Oh, geez." I made a face and put my beer down. "Let me dislodge that disturbing image. The last thing I want to think about is you and Kane bumping uglies." I stuck my tongue out at her and swam across the pool.

Kane was gorgeous, there was no denying that, but he was like a brother to me. Thinking about him and Jade… Ugh. No. Never. I'd rather endure Ida May's incessant sex talk than think about that.

Jade let out a soft giggle and floated on her back, staring up at the brilliant stars.

I hovered near the edge of the pool and watched the singer strum her guitar as she finished out her song. She was dressed in ripped jeans and a tight camisole tank top. But she didn't seem the least bit cold. She stood tall, her eyes closed as she focused completely on her song.

She was mesmerizing, with her long blond hair streaming out behind her and a rasp in her voice. Her pitch and tone were dead-on, so good she should've been a world-wide sensation.

I'd just turned and focused once again on the stars when I heard the high-pitched scream. Whirling, I caught sight of a person dressed in all black forcing the singer back toward the ship's railing. He had his hands around her neck, silencing her as he dragged her.

"Hey!" I cried, frantically swimming toward the ladder. "Stop. You're going to kill her!"

The attacker either didn't hear me or didn't care because he didn't even so much as flinch at my outburst. Using just one hand, he yanked her off her feet, squeezed her neck until her eyes were bulging, and then grabbed both her shoulders.

I was almost out of the pool when our eyes met. Her frantic ones pleaded into mine, and then without a word or even a struggle, the man in black threw her over the side.

"No!" I cried, sprinting toward the back of the ship,

dodging deck chairs and umbrellas as I went. A sharp pain stabbed at my foot, but I ignored it, my heart racing and panic flooding my body.

There had to be an alarm, someone to tell. They had to stop the ship. "Woman overboard!" I called belatedly and rammed into the railing. The man had disappeared and I was all alone, staring into the churning water below.

"Oh my god," I whispered into my hand. She was nowhere to be seen. "Help!" I screamed over and over again until I felt Jade's familiar arms circle me.

"Pyper, what's wrong. What happened?"

I focused on her, my mouth working as I struggled to form words.

"Deep breath now. What did you see?" She wrapped my robe around my shoulders and rubbed her hands up and down my arms.

"The singer. He… the man." My voice trembled through my chattering teeth. "He choked her and then threw her overboard."

Her brows drew together in confusion. "What singer?"

"The one who was playing the guitar." I frantically scanned the dark waters below. "We have to tell someone. They have to search for her."

"I didn't hear a singer," Jade said almost to herself.

"Does it matter? I saw it happen. Jade, we have to get help." I gripped the rail of the ship until my hands ached. "That man is dangerous."

She stepped back and frowned. "Are you sure that's what you saw?"

"Jade!"

She held her hands up. "I'm not trying to be difficult. We can get someone, but I think it's better if we go find Julius and Kane first."

I shook my head, an ache forming over my left eye as I pointed toward the water. "She's out there, and every second is critical." I took off running toward the doors that led to the bar we'd been in earlier, but before I could grab the door handle, Jade stopped me.

"Listen. I didn't see anything. I think what you saw wasn't real."

"Of course it was real." I shook her off. "I heard her singing and then she screamed when he attacked her."

She nodded. "I'm sure you did. But *I* didn't. I heard you scream and watched you scramble out of the pool. But I didn't hear or see anything else. And what's more, I didn't feel anyone but you."

Jade was an empath. Sensing other people's emotions was an everyday thing for her. She could block them out if she wanted to, but it took effort. If she hadn't been trying and she hadn't felt anyone but me, that could only mean one thing.

"No one was there."

"No one alive anyway," she added gently.

All the tension drained from my shoulders as realization hit. "They were ghosts."

She nodded slowly, her lips set in a frown. "I think you just witnessed an unsolved mystery."

"Huh?"

"Come with me." She grabbed my wrist and pulled me in a new direction, toward the doors that led to our staterooms. "I have something to show you."

Chapter 3

J ADE CROSSED HER stateroom—the one right next to the room
Julius and I shared—with a thick, spiral-bound binder. She'd
changed into jeans and a fitted T-shirt, and with her freshly
washed face, she looked like she'd just stepped out of a
cosmetics commercial.

I, on the other hand, had my hair tied up in a haphazard
bun and was wearing yoga pants and an old, faded Prince T-
shirt I'd gotten back in high school.

Sitting next to me on the couch, Jade flipped to the glossary
in the back and then to the page she was looking for. "Maximus
managed to obtain a dossier from the cruise line on all the
unusual activity that's ever happened aboard this ship. Kane
already took a copy to Julius."

"And you read this entire thing before you met me at the
bar?" I asked, my tone incredulous as I peered at the page.

She let out a small chuckle. "No, but I did flip through it. A
mysterious disappearance is kind of hard to miss."

"Yeah, I guess so." Right there at the top of the page was a
picture of the woman I'd seen singing near the pool. Her hair
was different, not long and flowing but short and shaved on one
side of her head. Even so, there was no doubt it was her. I

sucked in a tiny breath, both relieved I hadn't witnessed a live murder, and disturbed I hadn't realized I'd been watching an apparition. I'd had no idea.

"It says here her name's Vienna Vox. She was the lead singer of the Black Magic Witches, a band that was on the rise ten years ago before she mysteriously vanished." Jade grimaced and pointed to a passage below the woman's picture.

I read out loud. "Vox came from a long line of witches located on the Eastern Seaboard. She showed moderate ability with the craft."

"Of course she did," Jade said, irritation coloring her words as she got up to pace.

"So? Most everyone you know is a witch."

Jade was the leader of the New Orleans coven. Witches were her thing. Ghosts were mine. Seemed we were the perfect team for investigating whatever I'd witnessed.

"It's the black-magic part. She named her band Black Magic Witches. If she was dabbling in dark spells, we could be opening Pandora's box by poking into this."

"True, but if she was, I find it hard to believe she'd be so bold to advertise that fact in her band name." No one was that stupid, were they?

"One would hope." She reached into a plain paper bag sitting on the dresser, pulled out two fancy chocolate cupcakes, and offered me one. "How about a little pick-me-up before we go inform the men about our newest discovery?"

The corner of my mouth twitched into a smile. "Jade, my friend, I knew there was a reason I liked you."

✧   ✧   ✧

"IT'S AT THE end of the hall," Jade said.

We were on the main deck, heading toward the suite Julius and Kane were investigating, when a tall dark-haired girl stumbled out of her room with a bottle of Jack in her hand. She wore skintight leather pants, an illusion top with sparkling silver crystals, and matching silver boots. Black mascara ran down her makeup-coated face as she tried and failed to stay upright on her five-inch heels.

"Whoa," she cried out and grabbed for the door handle but went down in a heap anyway, the whiskey drenching the royal-blue carpet.

"Are you okay?" I asked, giving her a hand.

"Am I okay?" she asked in a smoky voice. Shaking her head, she stared up at me with the bluest eyes I'd ever seen. "No one's okay. Not anymore."

"I'm sure it isn't that bad," Jade said unconvincingly as she took a step back, carefully putting distance between them. No doubt the woman's volatile emotions were slamming into her. With booze-impaired inhibitions, the woman would be an open book and Jade would find it harder to block her out.

"Here." I clasped the woman's hand and pulled, tugging her up onto her feet. Her fingers gripped mine so tight I bit back a wince. Holy crow, she was strong. "Where are you headed?"

"Sound check." She slurred her words and swayed slightly when she pulled her hand from mine.

"You're putting on a show tonight?" I asked, giving Jade a look of alarm. This woman needed to sleep it off, not get on stage.

"Every night. I'm Muse, the lead singer for Unleashed."

"Right. Of course." Unleashed was headlining the ship's

entertainment for the week. They'd had a hit six or seven years ago but hadn't been heard from much since. No wonder they were playing cruise ships. "I'm Pyper, and this is my friend Jade."

Muse gave us a halfhearted nod and took a step back, leaning against the wall. The sound of a phone buzzing came from her back pocket. When she finally retrieved it, she let out a groan. "I'm late. And Jake's pissed."

She held the phone out. There was a text in all caps:

GET YOUR ASS DOWN HERE. NOW! OR WE'RE GIVING THE VOCALS TO TRIST.

"Trist's a hack singer. Can't do anything without Auto-Tune. But this time I think Jake might mean it." She turned her soulful eyes on me. "I can't even blame him. I've completely effed up."

Oh, get over yourself, Ida May's voice came from behind me. *At least your date didn't run off with another woman after you fondled his family jewels.*

I refrained from turning my head to acknowledge her arrival. It would only encourage her.

"Who are you?" Muse asked, staring over my shoulder.

I spun, seeing no one but Ida May.

You can see me? Ida May's dark eyes were huge with wonder.

Muse nodded. "Why wouldn't I?" She cast Ida May an appreciative glance, scanning her body from head to toe. "Damn, girl. Look at you. Sexy."

Ida May blushed and then preened as she floated past me and slipped her arm through Muse's. *So are you. Love the hair. But you're going to need to do something about that makeup.*

Raccoon eyes are never a good look.

Muse stumbled down the hall with Ida May beside her.

Jade gave me a questioning look.

"Ida May. Muse can see her. They have a mutual-admiration thing going on." I jerked my head toward them. "Come on. Let's make sure Muse makes it to the theater in one piece." Without going over the railing of the deck, I added silently, unwilling to let the drunk singer out of my sight.

After witnessing a girl—even if she had been a ghost—go overboard, I couldn't in good conscience let this one wander around unattended in her inebriated state. And Ida May as an escort did not count.

Jade nodded at me, indicating her agreement, but we stayed a few paces back.

"Muse is a mess of guilt," Jade whispered to me. "And fear."

I frowned. "I wonder what that's about."

Jade shrugged. "Could be anything."

We were silent as we followed the weaving Muse through the ship to the theater. Ida May kept up a running chatter about someone named Elias from the Green Parrot she'd been frequenting earlier, but I tuned her out, watching the woman. She was tall and lanky, with long, wavy, honey-blond hair, and even in her altered state, she had a kind of swagger only a rock star could pull off. Impressive.

She paused outside a door that read Staff Only and turned to look at us. "Want to see the fireworks?"

"No, I—"

"Yes." Jade cut me off.

"But, ah, Jade? Don't you think we should get back to Kane and Julius?" I asked, confused. Why did she want to watch the band do a sound check? Especially if the rest of the band was pissed?

She gave me a just-trust-me-on-this-one look and jerked her head toward the door. "It'll be like a private concert."

Cripes, Pyper, stop being a stick in the mud, Ida May added, draping her arm over Muse's shoulders. *Goodness, what I wouldn't do for a swig of that whiskey.*

"All you had to do is ask." Muse placed her hand right where Ida May's would be, and a crackle of magic sparked around them both. Then a brilliant light blinded me, sending me stumbling backward.

"What the—Whoa. You're a witch?" Jade exclaimed.

I blinked, clearing my vision. Then I blinked again, not believing my eyes. Right there in front of me was a solid Ida May, with the whiskey bottle tipped to her lips as she took generous gulps of the amber liquid.

Muse shrugged one shoulder. "I told you there would be fireworks… I meant literally. You have to see what we have planned for the show tomorrow night."

Ida May finally lowered the bottle and wiped her mouth with the back of her arm. "That's a damn fine spot of booze." She gripped the bottle and stared down at her body. "Now that's unexpected." She ran her hands over her chest and cupped her breasts, her eyes lighting up as she grinned. "I haven't felt these puppies in nearly a hundred years. They're holding up better than I expected."

Muse studied Ida May's breasts for a moment, then reached out and grabbed the left one. "Good size. Firm. Yeah, you got some nice assets."

The door whipped open, revealing a dark-skinned woman

with cropped red hair. Dressed in thread-worn jeans, a white tank top, and combat boots, the pixie-like woman crossed her arms over her chest and glared at Muse. "You coming inside anytime soon, or are you too goddamned drunk again?"

"Nah, she gave her liquor to me," Ida May said and swept past the angry woman.

"Trist," Muse said, her tone flat. "What's the matter? You having a hard time remembering the words again?"

Trist narrowed her eyes. "Go on, keep it up. Stella's on standby. All we need to do is give her a call. She'll be ready for next week's cruise within an hour's notice."

"I bet." Muse swept past her bandmate and called over her shoulder. "This way, girls. It's time to get the party started."

"Hell yeah! I'm ready." Ida May linked arms with Muse while Jade and I shared a grimace.

"I guess you're getting your way," I said to Jade. "We can't leave Ida May here unsupervised. There's no telling what kind of trouble she'll manage to get herself into."

Jade chewed on her lower lip. "I'd guess skinny-dipping. Or beer pong contests."

"I think she'd be more likely to be doing body shots. But you're on the right track." With both of us chuckling, we followed the band into the theater.

And right there on center stage was a woman I recognized. The one I'd seen go over the side of the ship less than an hour before. Vienna Vox.

Chapter 4

VIENNA'S COMMANDING PRESENCE filled the softly lit stage as she rocked slowly from side to side, her wild blond hair streaming out behind her as she belted out a melancholy tune, her voice flawless. Barefoot, wearing a lace camisole and a flowing black skirt, there was a powerful innocence about her that touched me deep in my soul.

I stilled, utterly mesmerized.

Her voice was sheer perfection, singing about forbidden love and a shattered heart. Tears stung my eyes while my chest ached with sudden sadness.

"Hey." A warm hand touched my bare arm.

I jumped and sucked in a gasp of air. "Jade. Goodness. Sorry."

"What the heck were you staring at?" Her brows pinched together as she scanned what must've appeared to be an empty wooden stage.

"She's here. Vienna. She's singing the saddest song I've ever heard."

"Really?" Her eyes widened, then narrowed as she watched Ida May try to charm the band. Muse, Trist, and two other rocker chicks were gathered near the front row with Ida May in the center playing an air guitar. "No one else appears to see her. Not even Ida May."

"She's there. I swear." Then, before Jade could say anything else, I took off for the stage, determined to try to speak to the ghost. To find out what had happened to her.

I sat in a plush, red velvet seat in the front row, right in front of her. And as I watched, a strange feeling came over me. Like I knew her somehow. As if we were connected in some way. Some way other than the mystical spell she was weaving with her song.

She's stuck on her own plane, Lily, one of my guides, said after materializing beside me.

"What's that mean?" I asked, keeping my eyes glued to Vienna. I couldn't seem to look away even if I wanted to.

She's not really here.

"Do you mean not really here on this ship and I'm seeing her through some sort of veil? Or not really here as in this is all in my head?" From the corner of my eye, I noted Jade was once again helping Muse stay upright, but she was keeping a close watch on me.

You're seeing her through some sort of veil. I believe she's in another reality, and we're getting a peek into wherever she actually is.

I sucked in a sharp breath. "You mean she could be somewhere like the shadow world, or even hell?"

Definitely not hell. The surprise in Lily's tone made me want to turn my head to look at her, but I couldn't. My gaze was glued to Vienna. *It's more like a waiting area or... as if she's stuck on an elevator, waiting for it to finally let her off.*

"She needs help then." It wasn't a question. I was already on my feet, heading for the stairs to get onto the stage.

"Pyper! Come over and meet the band," Ida May called. "They have a story about a roadie with a nine-inch—"

"Stop, you're ruining the punch line," one of the rockers said, cutting her off.

I ignored them all as I ran up the steps. Vienna had her gaze searing into me, tears streaming down her face. As they flowed, her singing turned darker and more ominous.

My heart was breaking and pain seared through my chest, making it hard to breathe. Sobs clogged at the back of my throat, nearly choking me. Once my feet hit the weathered stage, I took two steps and fell to my knees, the weight of grief crushing me.

Vienna held her arm out toward me as if she was reaching for me, the tears tracking down her cheeks.

Voices sounded behind me, but the words were jumbled. I couldn't comprehend anything except the turbulence shuddering through me, hurt and anguish consuming every cell. It was as if my heart had been ripped out and trampled, my trust not just broken but torn to shreds. A moan that sounded more like a wounded animal escaped my lips, and I clutched my chest, willing myself to not break into a million tiny little pieces.

"Pyper!"

A bolt of sweet magic hit me, coursing through my limbs like a soothing balm until finally it reached my chest, neutralizing the awful grief.

"Pyper?" the voice said again.

I blinked and looked up into Jade's frantic green eyes. Her strawberry-blond hair hung limply around her red face, sweat coating her skin. I glanced at the now-empty stage, noting

Vienna was gone.

"What happened?" I asked.

"Good goddess." Jade let out a heavy sigh and sat back on her knees.

"You freaked out, girl," Trist said. "You probably got a bad batch of whatever drug you took. Drug dealers can't be trusted. I can't tell you how many times that's happened to me. If they'd only legalize that stuff, then we wouldn't have to worry if anyone's cutting it with laundry detergent. Am I right?"

"I don't do drugs," I mumbled as I sat up, holding my pounding head. The bolt of magic Jade had dosed me with hadn't quite fixed everything.

"Right." Trist snickered.

"Not everyone lives off nose candy like you do, Trist," Muse said, sneering at her. "Can't you see she's sick? Don't be such a bitch."

Their arguing was making my head pound. "Jade, can you take me back to my room?"

"Of course." She helped me to my feet, keeping her arm around my waist as we left the stage. Tiny jolts of energy tickled my skin where she touched me.

"You don't have to do that, you know," I whispered to her.

"What? Hold you up?"

"That too. But I meant pump your energy into me. I can walk under my own steam." My body did appear to be fine. It was only my head that felt like it was going to explode.

"You know that's not going to happen," she said in a mat-ter-of-fact tone.

If the room hadn't been spinning, I'd have fought her on it. She was an empath, and giving away her energy would make her vulnerable. But because she was a white witch with a heart of gold, I knew she wasn't going to let this go. Not when she could do something about it.

"As soon as we get you back to the room, I'll fix that headache."

Of course she knew about that. She could probably feel the pain as her own just by touching me. "I'm sure ibuprofen will do the trick."

"Maybe." But she didn't sound convinced.

"Save your strength for the wussies who need it." I closed my eyes against the splitting pain and prayed I wouldn't vomit.

✧   ✧   ✧

LUCKILY THE CUPCAKE I'd had earlier managed to stay down, but it was a close call. Twice I'd felt the bile rise up in the back of my throat, and twice I'd sat against the wall in the hallway until my stomach stopped churning. It was a miracle we'd made it back to the room at all.

"You can't take these pills without something more substantial than beer and dessert," Jade said, picking up the receiver to the phone. "Food, then drugs."

I squinted up at her from my place on the bed. Even the lone light on the other side of the room was too much for me in my incapacitated state. "Just magic me. Or whatever it is you do to fix people."

She raised one skeptical eyebrow. "Less than five minutes ago, you said, and I quote, 'Save your strength for the wussies who need it.'"

I winced as the pounding over my eye intensified. "I was trying to be brave. I'm over it. Zap me. Give me a head transplant. Put me in a coma. I don't care. Just make this go away."

Her lips twitched as she replaced the phone receiver. "I think we can skip the coma… this time." Then her cool hands were on my forehead. Instantly my stomach settled, and the pain in my head went from excruciating to a dull ache.

"How did you do that?" I muttered, keeping my eyes closed, unwilling to move for fear the spell would break.

"I haven't done anything yet." Then she applied pressure with her fingertips, sweeping them from the center of my forehead out toward my temples. The masked pain lessened with each stroke of her gentle touch. And when I was so relaxed I thought I might drift off to sleep, I heard her mutter, "*Curare.*"

The pain roared back, making me bolt straight up in the bed, my breathing ragged. "Son of a—"

A high-pitched scream came from somewhere in the room just before the migraine suddenly vanished. It took me a moment to realize the scream belonged to me. I was too busy running my hands over my head, trying to make sure it hadn't actually exploded.

"Ohmigod! Pyper, I'm so sorry." Jade placed her hands over mine. "Where does it hurt? What did I do?"

"You tried to kill me, obviously," I said with a smile, brushing her hands away.

She frowned. "Why are you smiling? Were you…? Damn you, Pyper, if that was a joke, it wasn't the least bit funny." The bed jostled as she jumped up and glared at me.

I tentatively sat up, testing my now pain-free head. Then I shook it. "No, it wasn't a joke." It really was a marvel how energized I actually was considering her spell had felt like a freaking brain aneurysm. "I'm not sure that spell is one you want to keep as a staple in your toolbox. It hurt like a mother. But it did work... even if it did try to kill me."

She sank back down on the bed, her eyes round with concern. "It wasn't supposed to hurt. I've used it dozens of times on Kane and... crap." She hung her head.

"And your coven witches? People who have magic?" I guessed.

She nodded and grimaced again. "Sorry. I should've taken it down a notch or two. I was just so worried. The pain coming from you... I don't even know how you were able to walk back here."

"That makes two of us." I swung my legs over the edge of the bed and glanced around. "What happened to Ida May?"

"I'm not sure." She backed up and leaned against the dresser. "When I cast the spell to break whatever hold Vienna had on you, she vanished. I think it neutralized whatever Muse did to make Ida May human. She could've even been sent back to the café."

"Or somewhere else?" I said with a small shock of alarm. Ida May, while sometimes a pain, had become more than just our daily entertainment. Okay, maybe she was mostly just entertainment. But she was usually harmless and put a smile on my face. I'd even go so far as to say we were friends... as much as a human and a ghost could be friends anyway.

"I doubt it. She seems to be connected to you. If she did end up somewhere else, it'd be temporary at most."

A small shot of relief filled me. Ida May was like our mascot. If she was gone, I'd have to find myself another ghost. The image of Vienna sobbing in my café flashed in my mind and I shuddered.

No. Absolutely not. Any ghost of mine was required to be happy and have a sense of humor. No maudlin ghosts for *The Grind*.

"Everything okay? You looked for a second like you might pass out on me."

It was the memory of Vienna I supposed. "No. I'm good. Feeling great actually. Give me five minutes, then we'll go find the menfolk. See what trouble they've gotten themselves into this evening."

"I can hardly wait," Jade said dryly. "With the way this night has started, I wouldn't be surprised if we found them dealing with a dominatrix black-magic witch who was planning to use them both as her sex slaves."

I laughed. "Crazy rock stars and dominatrix witches. Sounds about right."

Chapter 5

JADE KNOCKED ON the door for room 1538 and waited. After a few moments, she rapped again, harder.

"Are they in there?" I asked her.

She nodded. "They're in a really good mood too."

"Party's over. The women are here," I called through the door.

Footsteps sounded from inside the stateroom, followed by the door opening. Kane waved us in, a satisfied smile claiming his face. "Hurry up. Julius is getting ready to cast a cleansing spell."

I swept past him, the faint scent of cleaning products and sea air assaulting my senses, and headed toward Julius who was standing next to the floor-to-ceiling sliding glass door that headed out onto the balcony. Every light was lit in the spacious room, illuminating the high-end décor—two leather couches, crystal light fixtures, a king-sized bed, extra plush carpet, and mirrors covering an entire wall. It was like a mini Vegas hotel room.

Behind me, I heard Jade ask, "You've found the culprit already?"

"Yeah." The door shut with a thump. "Sort of. Julius has

identified an old spell that's causing the havoc, and he's going to neutralize it. No demons this time." Kane draped his arm over Jade's shoulders, his posture more relaxed than I'd seen in weeks. Being a demon hunter, it must've been nice for him to get a small break.

"Good news." Jade ran her hand over her husband's arm and glanced our way, locking her gaze on Julius. "Want any help?"

"No way," I said, slipping my arm around my boyfriend's waist. Smiling up at him, I added, "She doesn't know her own strength, and I'd hate for anything to happen to you. I have plans for you later."

A gleam of interest flashed in his dark gaze. "Then I should definitely handle this one on my own."

Jade tsked. "For goddess's sake. Y'all make me sound like I'm some out-of-control newbie."

I peered at her, one brow raised. "We did just have that little headache incident."

Her face flushed and she responded with a sheepish grimace. "Right."

"What headache incident?" Julius asked, frowning. "Are you feeling okay?"

I nodded. "Yeah, I'm fine. I'll fill you in later. Nothing to worry about."

"What'd you find here?" Jade asked Julius. "The spell I mean."

He ran a hand over his forehead and wrinkled his brow. "It's a little hard to identify because it feels like it's been here for a long time, as if it's infested every inch of the room. Does that make sense?"

"Sure. Old spells can be like that. They really grab hold and become part of the environment," Jade said.

"Yes. Exactly. Only it also appears to be unraveling at the seams, becoming unstable. And that's possibly why guests have noticed an upswing in activity."

"How can you tell?" I asked, glancing around the room. There was nothing about it that seemed unusual to me. The moonlight was shining in through the windows, and had I not known about the black magic, I'd have been happy to sit down, prop my feet up, and enjoy the shimmer of light bouncing off the water.

Julius opened his mouth to answer but stopped when everything started to shake and a low rumble filled the room.

I stumbled, taken completely off guard, but Julius tightened his hold on my hand, keeping me from falling on my butt.

The rumble turned into more of a moan and faded away when the light near the bed flickered twice, then winked out.

Jade placed her hand on the wall, but she yanked it back immediately and stared at her palm as if she'd been bitten. "Damn. There's lots of unsettled energy in that spell."

Julius nodded.

"Emotional energy?" Kane asked her, his dark eyes narrowed as he ran a hand through his thick, dark hair.

"No. It's not that. It's like Julius said... unstable and invasive. Like the magic is so entwined in the room it has nowhere else to go, and it's breaking down. I imagine the effects of that are just as terrifying as the spell itself."

Another small rumble filled the room as tendrils of smoke arose from the middle of the bed.

My eyes widened. Holy fireballs. Things just got real. I

released my hold on Julius and backed up out of the way.

Julius waved his hand and ordered, "*Release!*"

The smoke vanished immediately, and the room settled.

"Nicely done," Jade said with a smile.

"Small illusions like that have been happening all night," Kane said.

Small illusions? The freakin' bed had been on fire. Though… there weren't any burn marks.

"All night?" I asked, trying to ignore the unease crawling all over my skin. "No wonder people were freaked out. If I hadn't been standing next to all of you badasses, I'd have bolted." The energy of the room was just wrong, and the sooner Julius broke the spell, the better. If it'd been my room, I'd have slept on a lounge chair near the pool.

The memory of Vienna Vox screaming just before she went over the edge of the railing flashed in my mind, and a shiver ran up my spine. Maybe I'd skip the pool area and head for one of the lounges.

"Okay, everyone out," Julius ordered.

"No way." Jade placed her hands on her hips. "What if you need help?"

"She's right. She should stay." I was in full agreement with Jade. Leaving Julius to deal with some old spell on his own felt reckless when there was a powerful white witch at his disposal. I crossed the room, grabbed Kane's arm, and tugged him toward the door. "Come on, big guy. Let's wait out in the hall while these two curse-breakers get their groove on."

"Only if there's a drink involved," Kane said and winked at Jade. No doubt the spell was a lot less concerning than the many black-magic witches and demons the pair had battled in the past. Because he was a lot less concerned than I was.

Jade smiled at us, but Julius's expression remained troubled.

I paused at the door and peered at him. "What is it?"

He frowned and shook his head. "I'm not sure. I thought I saw—"

The lights cut out, followed by another loud rumble and a flash of lightning across the ceiling. Everything went pitch-black. The room seemed to start closing in around me, making it hard to breathe. My thoughts jumbled, and I reached out, trying to steady myself. Red-hot, searing pain flashed through my palm the moment it connected with the wall.

"Ouch!" I cried, yanking my hand back at the same time Jade yelled, "It's getting worse!"

"Pyper?" Julius called out from somewhere in the darkness.

"I've got her," Kane said, wrapping a protective arm around me as he pulled me to his side.

"*Illuminate*!" Jade shouted. Floating orbs appeared in the room, giving the space an ominous glow.

I sucked in a sharp gasp. The walls were orange-red, the color of embers, and the paint was blistering as the room heated to unbearable levels.

Kane tightened his hold on me but kept his gaze glued to Jade. She and Julius were in the middle of the room, standing back to back, their arms raised in battle. Magic crackled at Jade's fingertips. But Julius stood stock-still, his eyes trained on the wall of mirrors across the room.

"What's happening?" I asked Kane in a hushed tone. Usually Jade was much more reactive to magical threats.

He shook his head. "I'm not sure."

Jade's long hair whipped around as she jerked her head to

look at Julius. "Do you feel that?"

"Yes." Julius didn't move, his body stiff with tension.

I squeezed Kane's hand, certain something terrible was about to go down. "We have to get out of here. All of us," I said to him.

Kane nodded but said, "They won't leave. You know that as well as I do."

I reached for the door but stopped when I noticed the gold discoloration on the normally silver handle. The heat had reached the door. We weren't going anywhere.

"The magic's embedded in the walls," Jade said.

But Julius shook his head and took a step away from her. "It's in the mirrors on the wall."

I followed his gaze and tightened my hold on Kane. "Holy hellfire. What is that?"

He frowned and shook his head. "Something a lot more evil than just a special effects spell."

No kidding. Fire raged in the mirror, the flames contorting from a solid sheet covering the mirror to a blazing fireball and then into an outline of an angry beast, its fangs bared and smoke streaming from its eyes.

Julius raised both arms straight out and started chanting something in Latin. Jade followed suit, and soon both had bright white magic spewing from their hands, aimed directly at the fire monster snarling at them in the mirror.

I was transfixed. The smoke stream dissipated, replaced by glowing amber eyes. The fangs retracted, and the giant monster head slowly morphed into something slightly more human. The room started to cool, and the walls returned to their off-white, neutral color, but the flames still roared as if the spell was retracting all its energy, saving it to fight the two witches.

"It's working," Kane said, trying to reassure me.

"Only if they manage to neutralize it," I said.

He gave me an odd look. "They will."

They always did, and there was no reason to believe otherwise now, but there was something about those amber eyes. They were watching me, and I felt as if the monster in the mirror was staring straight into my soul.

I wanted to run, to get the hell out of there. Be anywhere other than that room. There was only one other time in my life when I'd felt so exposed, so vulnerable. The memory of being trapped in another world while I'd been kept captive by an evil ghost flashed through my mind and made ice run through my veins.

Kane was right. Evil was trapped in that mirror. I could feel it in my soul.

"Now!" Julius cried.

The two witches joined their streams of magic as if they were a team straight out of *Ghostbusters,* and together they shouted, "*Resero!*"

The mass of fire tore from the mirror, once again taking the shape of the growling monster head as cries of rage filled the room. The white electric magic crawled all over the fire, engulfing the evil, coating it until all that was left were those piercing amber eyes that seemed to *know* me.

Fear clutched at my heart, making me ache to run. But I couldn't. I was frozen in place, unable to move as I fought for my sanity. Whatever was there wasn't Roy, the evil spirit who'd tortured me, but I couldn't shake the feeling that it was just as bad and wouldn't hesitate to come after me. Needing to do something, anything other than be a helpless bystander, I shouted, "Never again, you son of a bitch! Your hold is broken!"

I felt Kane turn his head and gaze down at me, but I couldn't tear my eyes from the monster. Instead, I tightened my fingers around his, letting him know I wasn't actually losing my mind.

The monster's eyes narrowed, piercing me with a glare, then widened in shock as the white magic finally swallowed the last of him. The magic instantly transformed into smoke and writhed in on itself as if the monster hadn't given up and was still trying to break free.

The four of us stood there watching until finally Jade said in a clear voice, "By the power of the New Orleans coven, I hereby banish you from this earth."

The smoke stopped, hovered in the air, and then slowly faded away, leaving the room in pristine condition as if nothing had ever happened.

"Whoa, I—" My words were cut off by a shimmer of light that surrounded Jade and Julius. "What's happening?" I asked Kane.

"Looks like the residual magic is looking for a home," he whispered, seemingly unconcerned.

"Is that normal?"

"It can be. That was a crap-ton of magic those two just freed. Think of it like a boomerang effect." He gave me a smile. I was sure he meant it to be reassuring. It failed.

I'd seen too much in the past few years to take anything for granted. But when the shimmering light touched both witches, they both grinned and opened their arms, welcoming the magic home.

"See," Kane said, pointing at Jade and her radiant smile.

"Yeah, I guess so." The knot in my chest started to unravel, and I moved toward them but stopped midstep. From the corner of my eye, I swore I saw a flash of light, an outline of someone right behind Julius. I blinked and peered at him.

Nothing.

Whatever it was had disappeared.

"Pyper?" Julius asked, holding his hand out for me. "What is it?"

"Nothing, I—" Shaking my head, I did my best to dislodge the fear that was still invading my chest. Roy had done a number on me, and for months afterward I'd jumped at my own shadow. That's all this was. Residual trauma. Whatever the evil spell had been, Julius and Jade had taken care of it. Neutralized. Gone. "I just thought I saw something. It must've been the lights."

Julius wrapped an arm around me and pulled me into him as Kane did the same to Jade.

Jade tilted her head and eyed me. "That was a little unusual. Seems your words were able to help with the spell a little bit."

I shrugged. "I don't know about that. It was probably just a coincidence. It's not like I have magic or anything."

"No," Jade agreed. "But you know a lot of this stuff feeds off intent. It's possible your energy helped."

Julius glanced from her to me, then shrugged. "Jade's right. It's possible."

Well, I didn't exactly want it to be. Being a medium was one thing, but a witch was entirely another. Working for the council or fighting off evil all the time sounded exhausting. I was quite happy at my café, thank you very much.

"I think it's time for a drink," Jade said, smiling up at her man.

I sucked in a breath, leaned into Julius, and nodded. "Make mine a triple."

Chapter 6

THE PARTY WAS in full swing at the One-Eyed Fish. Apparently it was the hot spot for passengers who wanted to get their groove on. Julius tugged me through the crowd as a high-energy tune blared from the surround sound and blue lights flashed in concert with the beat. I half expected the crowd to start producing glow sticks as they moved over the dancefloor.

Jade and Kane held hands and bent their heads together at the bar, her strawberry-blond hair contrasting against his dark locks. Their easy way with each other, their obvious love, had me aching for the intimacy they shared. I stopped short and turned to Julius. "Do you mind if we skip the drinks?"

He frowned. "Are you all right? Did something—"

I held up my hand, smiling. "I'm perfectly fine. I was just thinking that rather than spend the rest of the night with half the ship, I'd prefer to be back in our room... alone."

A glint of mischief sparked in his gaze. "Ms. Rayne, I can't think of anything I'd like better."

"Then let's go." I grabbed his hand and started leading him back through the crowd.

When we made it into the main corridor, he paused. "You don't want to let Jade and Kane know we're turning in?"

I placed both hands flat on his well-defined chest and stared up at him. "They'll figure it out."

His dark eyes smoldered with heat as he gazed down at me. Tucking a runaway lock of hair behind my ear, his voice turned husky as he said, "I've been waiting a long time for a night alone with you."

"I know. Me too."

Using his thumb, he gently caressed my temple. "You're sure? I don't want to take advantage of you."

I stifled an amused chuckle. You could take the man out of the 1920s, but you couldn't take the twenties out of the man. "Trust me when I say I'm not the one who's going to be taken advantage of."

His hand tightened on my hip as he pulled me closer. "Don't say things you don't mean."

"I wouldn't dream of it," I whispered as I rose onto my tiptoes and brushed my lips over his.

He let out a small murmur of appreciation and slid his hand around to cup my bottom.

A ripple of pleasure skirted through me as he teased the seam of my lips with his tongue. I pressed myself against him and opened my mouth to his, savoring the faint taste of the wine we'd had hours before at our interrupted dinner. Everything started to tingle, and I deepened the kiss, suddenly overtaken by the ravenous hunger I harbored for this man.

"Damn, Pyper," he said against my lips, his breath already short. "You're the sexiest thing I've ever seen in my hundred years."

"Room. Now," I demanded and kissed him again, my tongue laving at his in slow, luxurious strokes.

He didn't hesitate. In one swift movement, he lifted me into his arms as if I weighed nothing and strode down the corridor.

"I could've walked," I said, already undoing his tie.

"This was faster." He caught an empty elevator before the doors closed and set me on my feet just as he hit the button for our floor.

"Hmm, really?" I closed the small distance between us, snaked my hand around to the back of his neck, and pulled his head down slightly so our lips met once again.

His tongue was hot, insistent, and sent shivers of desire everywhere with each demanding thrust against mine.

I melted and the world around us fell away. All I knew was him, his lips, his fingers digging into my flesh, and the heat radiating from him. And I gladly would've stayed right there, molded to him, had it not been for the chime of the elevator indicating we'd reached our floor.

The doors opened and a polite cough, followed by an irritated clearing of the throat, interrupted us.

Julius released me but immediately slipped his hand into mine, tugging me out of the elevator. He mimed tipping his hat at the older lady who was staring at him, her cheeks flushed bright red. Her male companion glared at us through his wire-rimmed glasses.

"Now that's what passion looks like, Carl," I heard the woman say, wistfulness in her tone. Then she turned on him and added, "You should take notes before I decide to move to one of those assisted-living homes. I hear those places are full of randy old buggers.

"Pearl!" he admonished. "Don't be crass."

"I'd rather be crass and satisfied by a lover. If I have to reach for that vibrator one more time—"

The doors closed on the couple, cutting off her next words.

I giggled, loving her sass.

Julius glanced down at me. "That's one thing you won't need tonight."

Grinning, I leaned into him. "Oh? You have plans for me?"

"You have no idea." He was so fast opening the door I didn't even register the key card. Then we were alone.

Finally.

We both stilled, gazing at each other as if taking in the moment.

"You're the most beautiful woman I've ever laid eyes on," Julius said.

I felt a pleased smile tugging at my lips as I moved in, my hands reaching for the buttons on his shirt. "I hope that's not the only thing you plan to lay on me."

He brushed his thumb over my cheek, the moment so tender it almost brought tears to my eyes.

"Stop that," I whispered as I tore my gaze from his, not quite ready for all he had to offer. That look… it held promises and happily-ever-afters. That was something that happened for women like Jade. Not me, the girl who came from a broken home and had put herself through college by managing a strip club. Not that I was ashamed of anything I'd had to do. But I'd seen enough of the real world to know that things usually didn't end with promises of forever. Not promises that were kept anyway.

"Why?" He ran that same thumb lightly over my lips. "Your skin is so smooth. Flawless like porcelain."

"It's not…" I tilted my head to gaze up at him and got lost

in the intensity staring back at me.

"Not what?" He brushed his lips over mine, the heat of them nearly bringing me to my knees.

Yes, my body screamed and swayed into him. All my previous thoughts vanished as I pushed his shirt off his shoulders and ran my fingers over his chest, reveling in his perfection. "Goodness. It's a crime you ever get dressed in the morning."

He chuckled and slipped his hands under my shirt, caressing the bare skin at the bottom of my ribcage. "Something tells me I'm going to be saying the same about you."

Now this place, the flirtatious one right before we really got down to business, was right in my wheelhouse. I took a step back, putting just enough distance between us that he could no longer reach out and touch me.

He extended his arm and took a step forward, but I held my hand up and danced backward just a touch.

I shook my head while giving him my most seductive smile. "No touching. Not yet. I want to show you what you've been missing these past few months."

His eyes darkened with desire, and as I slowly inched my T-shirt up, revealing my midriff, he licked his lips.

Holy smolder. It was all I could do to not just throw myself at him. I wanted that tongue—

"Pyper?" a high-pitched voice said in my ear, followed by a loud popping sound as Ida May materialized beside me.

"What the hell?" I glared at the floating ghost. "Ida May! We're in the middle of something here."

She glanced from me to Julius, let out a low whistle, and fanned herself with one hand. "I'd say. Damn, that man's hot."

Julius shrugged his shirt back on and fastened one button,

appearing very uncomfortable with Ida May's attention.

I pointed toward the door. "You can leave now."

She shook her head, her wild dark curls bouncing around her face. "Oh, no. I can't leave here without you. There's a problem."

I sighed and adjusted my shirt, making sure I was covered. "What kind of problem?"

"There's a ghost down at the Midnight Chocolate Bar. I need you to help me get rid of him."

"Him?" I raised a skeptical eyebrow.

"What ghost?" Julius asked, moving to stand next to me. He put his arm around my waist and pulled me close until I was tucked firmly against him.

Ida May stared at us and then shook her head. "You two make me want to gag. When did you get so… touchy-feely? Don't you think it's a little rude to do that in front of me? I mean, it has been forever since I've felt a man pressed up against—"

"Ida May, why are you here?" I demanded, not wanting to hear about the last time she did anything with a man.

"Right." She zoomed toward the door. "Like I was saying, there's a ghost at the chocolate bar, and if someone doesn't stop him, it's likely he's going to take over someone's body."

"What are you talking about?" I was already tugging Julius toward the door.

"You'll see. Hurry, before it's too late." Ida May disappeared again, this time sailing right through the door.

I let out a small sigh of frustration and glanced up at Julius. "Rain check?"

He placed his hand on the small of my back, his touch

easing the dread already forming in the pit of my stomach. "Count on it. Now let's go check out the chocolate bar. Even if Ida May is full of BS, at least we can pick up some dessert for… later."

The way he looked at me when he said *later* had me ready to tear my underwear off right then and there. But I managed to put the thought out of my mind as I followed him out of the room.

✧   ✧   ✧

The sign posted outside the large ballroom read:

Welcome to Illusion's Adults Only
Midnight Chocolate Bar.
Party from midnight till dawn.

I glanced at Julius. "I'd bet some kids are pretty upset right now."

He chuckled and pointed at another sign that indicated there was a children's version just down the hall. "Seems the powers that be have already thought of that."

Someone opened the door leading to the kids' area, and shrieks of delight filled the hallway.

"Thank the gods for small favors," I said, grateful that if I couldn't be alone with Julius, at least we could enjoy a grown-up activity together.

"There you are!" Ida May flew through the air straight at me. "Hurry up. If you don't do something soon, some poor unsuspecting bloke is going to get a rude awakening when Bootlegger is suddenly in charge of his manbits."

"Bootlegger?" I asked.

"Elias 'Bootlegger' Jamison. Keep up." She glided back through the double doors into the ballroom.

Julius and I glanced at each other, his skeptical look mirroring my own internal feelings.

I sighed. "Let's just get this over with so we can get back to our scheduled programing."

He tightened his grip on my hand and nodded. "Ida May just took the top billing on my 'most likely to be exorcized' list."

I laughed. "Normally I'd fight you on that, but if she interrupts sexy time again, I'll call the priest myself."

He grinned down at me, then sobered as he pierced me with his stare. My breath caught and I automatically leaned into him, more than ready for whatever he was planning.

"Holy hormones!" Ida May shrieked. "Get a grip, horndogs. There's a ghost planning some creepy crap that you need to stop."

Julius and I both took a step away from each other. I instantly felt empty. Alone. Almost as if I'd lost something important. I eyed him as he turned to Ida May.

He pulled at his shirtsleeves, straightening them as he stared at her, all traces of his earlier annoyance gone. "What is this about a rogue ghost?"

"This way." She weaved her way through the crowd, this time glancing behind her to be sure we were following.

Chapter 7

INSIDE THE BALLROOM, all the waitresses were dressed in short skirts, thigh-high boots, and bustiers that showed more cleavage than a romance-novel cover. The waiters wore skintight black pants and suspenders... no shirts. They were all gorgeous, sexy, and perfectly groomed, as if they were ready for a photoshoot.

One of the waitresses glided by, offering us champagne or Irish coffees. We both declined, preferring to keep our wits about us if there was a troublemaker ghost we'd have to deal with.

I glanced up and pointed at the banner hanging from the ceiling. It read: *Adult Night Chocolate Extravaganza, where the desserts are just as naughty as you are.*

"This is... not what I was expecting," Julius said.

I chuckled. "Me neither, but at least it promises to be entertaining."

We moved forward, the crush of people making me feel slightly claustrophobic. They were all crowded in front of a makeshift stage filled with a half dozen stainless steel tables and cooking equipment. Five of the tables had people in white bakers' jackets and chef hats. The sixth table was empty.

"Look." Ida May pointed to the station on the far left. "See him? He's hovering over the chocolate fountain, waiting for his opportunity."

I squinted, spotting a small man with a wide smile. He was busy arranging his mixing bowls and laughing at something a woman in the crowd had said. "You mean the very-much-alive human baker?" I asked, not bothering to hide my mild irritation.

"Behind him!" Ida May waved her arms out in front of her, her movements bordering on frantic.

I moved to the right and finally the ghost in question came into view right beside the vat of liquid chocolate. He was tall, thin, had long scraggly hair, and wore a midlength leather coat that looked like it hadn't been cleaned in over a hundred years. If he hadn't had a scar that ran from his eye down his cheek, he'd actually have been very handsome with his angular jawline and vibrant eyes.

I frowned. "He appears harmless."

"You don't understand. I told him about how Muse spelled me and that for a few glorious minutes I was solid, a real live person again. And he got very excited, started talking about how he knew a way to enter a human body, you know—possess someone. Not just turn solid on his own." Ida May scowled up at the stage. "Do you have any idea what he plans to do if he pulls this off?"

I shook my head.

She turned and pointed to an elegant woman with her blond hair piled on top of her head, standing off to the side of the stage. "Her. He wants to do her."

"Oh, for the love of—" I stared at Ida May for a moment.

"You know that sounds crazy, right?"

She locked gazes with me, her expression deadly serious. "I'm not crazy, Pyper. If he ends up in solid form, he's going to try to spend the night in another woman's bed. I can't have that. We made plans. The bastard." She cast a scowl at Bootlegger. "Now go up there and stop him."

Holy hell. This was all about her losing her man to another woman. Of course it was. What else did I expect from Ida May? I had half a mind to just turn around and leave, but if the ghost really did have some way of possessing another person, I couldn't. I had to do what I could to stop him, because gah! Taking over someone's body was the ultimate invasion. Standing by and letting it happen was unacceptable.

"You have to get up there. Stop him. Do something!" Ida May flew up to the stage, pointed her finger in Bootlegger's face, and started yelling at him as if they were an old married couple. Then she said something about his lack of morals and human decency, restoring my faith in her.

He just gave her a cocky smile and then eyed a group of male passengers as if deciding which would be the best host.

"She sure didn't waste any time finding herself a man, did she?" Julius asked.

I shook my head. "She certainly has a knack for drama."

"Hello, ladies and gentlemen!" The blond event coordinator Ida May had just pointed out made her way to the center of the stage, holding a microphone. She wore a lavender silk dress that hugged all her curves, accented with impossibly high silver heels. "Hi, y'all. I'm Maggie, and I'll be your host for the evening."

"Hi, Maggie!" the crowd said in unison as if they'd been

prompted.

Bootlegger, already an expert at ignoring Ida May, floated right beside Maggie, staring at her wolfishly. The very idea that he might have a body soon and a way to hit on her turned my stomach.

"I hope you're enjoyin' your first evening on the ship," she said, her Southern accent charming the crowd. "We have lots of fun in store for you tonight. Our bakers are here to show you the wilder side of the sweet treats we love so much. Nothing is off-limits. The naughtier, the better, we like to say!"

The crowd cheered, more than a couple of people making suggestive hand gestures and comments. Bootlegger joined in by reaching out and grabbing at Maggie's butt. She jerked and glanced over her shoulder, but when she saw nothing, she composed herself and turned once again to the crowd with an easy smile.

She held up a glass of champagne in a toast. "We have only the finest chocolate and spirits. By the end of the hour, our bakers will present their creations and you, the audience, will vote on the most creative. And while we wait, we'll have tastings and raffle drawings. But first, we need one more contestant. Someone from the crowd to keep things interesting. Now, who wants to volunteer?"

Hands rose instantly, followed by cries of, "Pick me! Pick me!"

I had to admit, the cruise ship sure knew how to throw a fun party.

Julius nudged my arm. "Volunteer."

"What? Me? Why?"

"Because, even if Ida May is crazy, there's still a ghost on that stage wreaking havoc. You could have your guides talk to him, or even just keep an eye on him in case he really does know how to possess someone. It's not unheard of, you know."

I did know. A spirit had possessed Jade once. She'd known what was happening but had been powerless to stop it. The trauma had taken weeks to get over. Julius was right. I had to do something. "Yeah, okay. But you better be ready to act at the first sign of trouble."

He nodded. "I'm not going anywhere." He glanced down at me with a mischievous smile. "Now go up there and make some inappropriate cupcakes. I can't wait to see what you come up with."

I chuckled and raised my hand high. We were right in front now, and as the hostess was scanning the crowd, I noticed Ida May beside her, whispering in her ear. At that moment, Maggie locked eyes with me, and cried, "Ahhh, I think we've found our volunteer."

Holy crow. Had Maggie actually heard Ida May? She hadn't acknowledged her at all, but it was clear she'd homed in on me as Ida May spoke to her. It had probably been some mystical ghost thing.

"Looks like someone could use a little encouragement," Maggie said, egging the crowd on.

They responded instantly, raising their glasses and chanting, "Go. Go. Go."

"Yes!" I cried out, mimicking the excitement of the crowd. If I was going to do this, it was best if I did it right.

"Come on up here, darlin'," Maggie drawled in her thick Southern accent, the kind that sounded more Tennessee than Texas.

I gave Julius one last look before I climbed up onto the stage to wild applause. Bootlegger turned his attention to me, cast his gaze up and down before leering at me. Staring him dead in the eye, I mouthed, *Don't even think about it.*

Surprise replaced his pervy expression. "You can see me."

I nodded once and gave him a warning look as I whispered, "Behave, or I'll have you exorcised."

"She'll do it too!" Ida May chimed in with her arms crossed over her chest.

The old ghost let out a loud laugh, then sobered as he glared at Ida May. "Go away. I've got my eye on something less… aged."

"Please," Ida May shot back. "No one here knows how to pleasure a man more than—"

Their argument was drowned out when Maggie put an arm around my shoulders and asked, "What's your name, sweetheart?"

"Pyper," I said into the microphone, grateful for the distraction from Ida May and Bootlegger.

The crowd shouted back, "Hi, Pyper!"

"Excellent! Now, you know the rules?"

I shook my head.

"Ohhh, a virgin!" She raised her hand to the crowd and moved her finger as if it were a conductor's wand. "On three. One, two—"

The crowd erupted into the chorus of Madonna's hit song.

I laughed, thoroughly enjoying myself.

"Very nice," Maggie said to the crowd. "I think a few of you have a future in the music industry." Then she turned to me. "Okay, you have one hour to make the most entertaining chocolate creation you can think of. The winner gets an all-expenses-paid trip for two to the eastern Caribbean. Now, I have to warn you. This is an adult party. Past winners have all been adult themed. So unless you're making humping bunnies, cute animals aren't gonna cut it." She glanced out at the crowd. "Am I right, guys?"

"Right!" they answered back.

I stared at the fully engaged crowd and started to wonder just how many had taken this cruise before. Maybe some of them were staff to get the party going.

"Got it, Pyper?" she asked.

"Got it. I assume all the ingredients that are laid out are available?" I asked as she walked me to my station. I was assigned the table between the short round man I'd spotted earlier and a tall thin woman. She had bright pink hair, a tattoo of a peacock on the back of her neck, and wore an all-purple boho-chic dress.

"Yep. Anything you find is acceptable. Even if your neighbor already claimed it. This is a full-contact sport."

Well, okay then.

"We'll start in just a few minutes."

She left me to my table and walked to the center of the stage, once more engaging the crowd. I took stock of my station: unsalted butter; unsweetened chocolate; semisweet chocolate; white chocolate; eggs; flour; and three different kinds of sugar: white, powdered, and brown. There was vanilla, a spice rack, nuts, spirits, and other herbs and infusions. Behind me was the giant fountain that kept churning the chocolate.

"He's already up to no good," Ida May said from behind me.

I turned my back on the crowd and prayed the other contestants couldn't hear me when I asked, "What are you talking about?"

She gave me a conspiratorial look and pointed into the pool of liquid chocolate in the fountain.

I peered over the edge and spotted an outline of a face with two ghostly eyes staring back at me. "Holy hell."

"You can say that again. He's contaminating all that fine chocolate," Ida May said.

I doubted that, being that he didn't actually have a form. But a face floating in the liquid was certainly creepy enough. "When did this happen?"

"Just now. One moment he was arguing with me, and the next he was diving into the chocolate." She pursed her lips as she watched him blink. "I kinda like it. I always was one for getting dirty."

"Oh geez. I did not need to know that," I said under my breath. I smiled at the boho lady beside me when she eyed me with suspicion.

"Just sayin'." Ida May grinned. "For someone from New Orleans, you sure are uptight."

I rolled my eyes. "Thanks for the input."

"Okay, bakers. Ready to create?" Maggie asked.

The other five pumped their fists in the air and yelled, "Ready!"

I followed suit, a step behind everyone, already making a name for myself as the loser.

"Then start your creations!"

Chapter 8

A LOUD BELL chimed, and everyone started running around like chickens with their heads cut off just the way they did on the reality TV baking shows. I took a small step back, making sure I was out of everyone's way.

"Better get on it," Boho Lady said. "If you don't start grabbing ingredients, they're going to be all gone."

I looked back at the ingredient table and realized she was right. Keeping one eye on the vat of chocolate, I hurried to the table and started grabbing everything I'd need for Jade's famous cream cheese chocolate chip cupcakes. It was just about the only thing I could think of off the top of my head. How I was going to make them adult themed, I had no idea. But it was a start.

No one went for any liquid chocolate.

That was good news, for now.

"Keep an eye on Bootlegger," I told Ida May while my back was turned to the crowd. "If he leaves the chocolate, or anyone takes any, let me know."

"You got it, partner."

I glanced at her. She gave me a wide smile and nodded, obviously pleased with herself. Chuckling, I crossed the stage, turned my assigned oven to 375, then got to work on the batter.

In no time, I had the cupcakes ready to go and in the oven.

The man on my right was busy fondling the modeling chocolate. I peered at the small shapes and tilted my head to the side, trying to register what they were. Then when he inserted a skewer into the bottom of one and held it up for inspection, the lightbulb went off. The curved, phallus-shaped chocolate pop was a little on the small side though. And I didn't care what anyone said: size did matter, especially when it came to chocolate. I snickered, aware I was behaving like a twelve-year-old boy.

"So obvious," Boho Lady muttered from my other side. "There's always one making a life-sized model of their junk."

I couldn't help it. I snorted a laugh.

She smiled at me, her brilliant green eyes sparkling with mischief. She was busy chopping off sections of a rectangular cake, shaping it into something I couldn't quite make out.

"It's a torso," she said, with a wink.

She was going full on *Cake Wars* with her creation. Impressive.

I pulled out modeling chocolate and went to work on cutting out perfectly round circles. Once they were placed on a wax sheet, I grabbed a couple of tubes of decorating icing and piped on cute little bikini tops and bottoms, alternating each one so I'd have an equal number.

Boho Lady glanced over and gave me a nod of approval. "Those will go over well. Not as good as this though." She waved a hand at her cake, which was now covered in fondant.

Whoa. In the short time she'd been working, she'd transformed the basic chocolate cake into a perfectly-sculpted replica of eight-pack abs, narrow hips, and low-slung blue jeans with the button open. "Dang, girl, you've got skills."

A satisfied smile claimed her lips. "I might have been practicing."

That seemed like a lot of effort for a free cruise, considering she was already on this one. But who was I to judge? Some people were just competitive.

"Pyper!" Ida May squealed from behind me. "He's on the move."

I turned, noting a splash of melted chocolate on the floor. "Who took the chocolate?"

"Her." She pointed across the stage at a voluptuous redhead. "That hussy leaned over the chocolate, giving him an eyeful of her girls, and that was enough. As soon as she took a quart of the chocolate, he followed her. I just knew he was a two-timing scoundrel."

Two-timing? Hadn't she just met him an hour or two ago? I shook my head. Her shenanigans weren't the point. I shifted my gaze to the redhead. She was holding a bottle of rum in one hand and a tall, slender double shot glass in the other.

Bootlegger was hovering over the open bottle of rum, licking his lips.

I frowned. What was he—

Then he moved. In a flash he evaporated into smoke and dove straight into the bottle. A small amount of rum bubbled out of the top and dribbled down the side.

Without thinking, I hurried over to the woman, my hand outstretched, reaching for the bottle.

"Whoa." She jerked the bottle to her chest, cradling it against her bosom. "Sorry, honey. You're too late. This is mine." She winked. "I can't make my special rum-and-cherry balls if someone else is hogging the rum."

Before I could answer, she turned back around to the crowd as if I were dismissed and started lining up her double shot glasses.

Crap.

Bootlegger was actually in that bottle.

Maggie's voice boomed through the sound system. "Looks like we have a little competition when it comes to the spirits."

I turned, my eyes wide. How did she know—?

"Only one person can use the rum," she said to me, not unkindly. "It's always a popular item when we do the Bake-Off. Perhaps the amaretto? Or Irish cream?"

Oh. Of course she meant the alcohol, not Bootlegger. I sighed, wondering if I should even do anything at all. He was just a ghost, not a witch. He'd need magic to invade someone's soul. Right?

Just then I glanced over at the redhead. She was pouring the rum into the eight shot glasses as if she were an expert bartender, never breaking the flow of the liquid until each glass was filled.

Silvery ghost matter slid in and out of the bottle and then settled, and a trail of matter flickered from the top like a smoke signal. It appeared Bootlegger was quite happy wallowing in his rum. Heck, if I'd been a ghost for the past however many years, I might like it there too.

The buzzer indicating my cupcakes were done went off, and I rushed to pull them out of the oven. As I was positioning them on the cooling rack, the redhead smiled at the crowd and raised the bottle high toward the audience. "Who wants a drink?" she called.

Hands rose in the air, followed by two enthusiastic men jostling for position at the front of the stage.

She eyed them. "Aren't you boys cute?"

"Drink, drink, drink," the crowd chanted.

I had my eyes glued to the rum, and my throat went dry when I saw the silvery substance float out of the bottle, hover there, and then zip back down. What would happen if someone drank that?

"You!" Redhead pointed at the man directly in front of her. He was tall and had wide shoulders and long, muscular legs. With short blond hair and a clean-cut image, he sported a typical college-football-player look. He reached out for the bottle almost as if in slow motion while I ran forward.

"Wait!" I cried.

But the crowd was too loud, and no one was paying any attention to me. Not that they would've cared anyway. I'd already been told the rum was off-limits to me.

"Give it up," Boho Lady said, moving to stand next to me as we watched the spectacle go down. "You're cute, but you have nothing on Miss Curves over there. A hundred bucks says she wins based solely on her cleavage. She could pour shots of booze and serve chocolate kisses as a side and still win this competition. It's always about the cleavage, dear."

I frowned, eyeing the football player as he waved his arms, igniting the crowd to cheer louder. "Then why are you here?" I asked, leaning in close so she could hear me.

She pointed to a person standing off to the side, pen in hand as he scribbled notes in a notebook. "Reporter for *Chef Magazine*. If I can get a mention there, sales will triple. We see it all the time."

"I see." I stared at her perfect cake, the one that looked like a flawless replica of a romance novel. She'd done some sort of shading to give the abs definition and had added the logo of a popular publisher off to the side for effect. It was nothing short of amazing.

"Do you? Why are you here? The free trip?" She snorted, clearly discounting my chances of winning.

"Uh, no. I just got roped into doing this. I don't really care one way or another."

"That explains why you're standing around looking like a lost puppy." She shoved some more modeling chocolate into my hands. "Here, make something. Anything. Otherwise you look like an idiot standing there, gaping at Scarlett O'Hara over there."

I took it just to appease her. But she had distracted me from the rum bottle.

Football-player guy was standing on the stage now next to Scarlett, holding the bottle high in the air.

Ida May was flying around them, wringing her hands as she cried, "No! Don't do it. Bootlegger, get out of that bottle right now. If you even think about having sex with this… this… harlot, that's it. We're done. That thing I said I'd let you do? Forget it. The offer is off the table."

Something stirred in the bottle, then I heard the sound of gargled laughter echo through the room. It was so loud I cringed and wanted to cover my ears. But glancing around, it was clear no one else but Ida May and me had heard anything.

"Bootlegger!" She whirled and turned to me. "Do something. He's going to make his move!"

I stood there, totally helpless. What exactly was I supposed to do? Knock the bottle out of the guy's hands? Mr. College Football had to have at least a hundred pounds on me. I didn't stand a chance.

Turning to the crowd, I spotted Julius. He was busy staring at the football player with an almost bored expression. But then the cheering crowd broke out into applause, and Julius's eyes widened. I turned and stared at Scarlett and Mr. Football. He had the rum tipped to his lips, the bottle bathed in a glowing amber light.

I let out a gasp.

Magic.

There was no other explanation.

And when Football Guy finally tore the bottle away from his lips, he gave Scarlett a crooked grin and his blue eyes darkened and then shifted to brilliant green. It was exactly the same expression I'd seen on Bootlegger's face just before he'd jumped into the vat of chocolate. He bowed slightly to Scarlett. "Thank ye, my lady. It's been over a hundred years since I've felt the sweet burn of the spirits in my throat."

She giggled, enjoying his performance.

His gaze turned wolfish as he wrapped an arm around her waist and tilted her back. "And even longer since I've tasted anything so fine."

Then Bootlegger closed the distance and kissed her.

Chapter 9

"OH, HELL!" I covered my mouth, afraid to call attention to myself, but I needn't have worried. The crowd erupted into catcalls and wolf whistles, drowning me out. I stood a few feet from the pair, frozen with indecision. My instinct was to tear them apart, but by the way they were tightly wrapped around each other, I had little hope of success.

"Do something!" Ida May cried, flying around me in a state of agitation.

"Like what?" It wasn't like I knew either of them. I couldn't just pull one of them away. Heck, Scarlett was even returning the kiss with full enthusiasm. But I couldn't do nothing. The poor college guy had been possessed. Even if he was okay with making out with a stranger, he wasn't in control, and that was all kinds of wrong.

"Make something up. Or get Julius to zap them. I don't know." She darted away, yelling at Bootlegger, though the pirate paid her no mind.

Zapping them wasn't a bad idea. I glanced over at Julius. He was staring at the spectacle with his eyebrows raised and a small amused smile on his face. Clearly he hadn't realized Bootlegger had taken over. I'd have to find a way to get to him if I was going to have his help.

You don't need Julius, Lily, one of my guides, said as she materialized beside me. Her bright red hair curled around her face, highlighting her striking gray eyes. She was young for a ghost, maybe midthirties, and usually soft-spoken. *You have the power to dispel him all on your own.*

"How's that?" I asked, no longer worried about anyone overhearing me. The crowd was either too hopped up on sugar or too drunk to worry about anything I was doing. Especially when Scarlett and Bootlegger were giving them an after-hours show.

He's just a visitor in that man's body. Possession takes a powerful spell, much more powerful than the transfer spell Bootlegger used.

"So he did use a spell. Was he a witch before he died?"

Lily nodded. *Not a very powerful one. But a witch, nonetheless.*

I glanced at Julius again. He was now staring at me, his brows furrowed. He'd noticed me talking to myself, though I was certain he knew I was talking to either one of my guides, Ida May, or Bootlegger himself.

"How do I dispel him?" I asked Lily, keeping my eyes on Julius.

You'd have to pull him out.

"How?"

She gave me a wry smile. *You have to suck him out.*

"What?" I turned and stared her in the eye, horrified. "You mean like a succubus sucks a soul?"

She nodded, already fading away, and just as she disappeared again, I heard her add, *It's not as bad as it seems. You'll see.*

Like hell. No way was I putting my lips on some stranger. Or gads, sucking ghost matter from them. Especially Bootlegger. A shudder ran through me. What if he decided to take up residence in me? The thought of Julius kissing me with Bootlegger as the third wheel made my stomach roll. Nope. Not now. Not ever. I needed Julius for this one.

I moved to jump off the stage, intending to grab Julius, but the crowd was starting to grow as more people poured into the room. A good portion of them were holding specialty cocktails and wearing feathered boas, a sure sign they'd just come from another bar, the Mardi Gras Lounge. What did the ship do? Make an announcement? Because suddenly the place was packed.

"You better hurry," Boho Lady said breathlessly as she pushed past me, reaching for a pair of wineglasses. "Five minutes until voting starts."

Crap. They likely *had* made an announcement. Julius was crowded in on all sides in the middle of the room. I tried to motion to him, to get him to join me, but he was turned around, facing the entrance instead of the stage.

What was he doing?

"Two-minute warning!" Maggie announced into the microphone. "Place your creations on the front table for judging."

I glanced at my table and groaned. I still had some work to do on my cupcakes. Not that it mattered. I didn't care about winning, only my pride. I had a reputation to uphold after all. It wouldn't be good business if I came in last place in a baking contest. The Grind was known for delicious pastries. If the *NOLA Times* picked up the story, I couldn't afford to look like an amateur.

I kept one eye on Scarlett and College Guy while I hurried to place my premade bikini tops and bottoms fondant onto my cupcakes. The cream cheese filling had created an indentation in the center, causing a sad sagging situation right in the middle. I grimaced. If I'd had more time, I'd have filled that section with caramel or more cream cheese, but there was no fixing it now. I'd never win this contest, but at least I had something to show for it.

Scarlett was busy arranging her rum shots with chocolate rum balls on one side and chocolate-covered cherries on the other. "I call it the Love Shot," she said to me conspiratorially as I placed my tray of cupcakes on the table.

I gave a noncommittal nod and eyed Mr. College Guy. His hungry, bright green eyes—Bootlegger's eyes—were locked on her butt.

"Twenty bucks says these beauties are the winners," my round neighbor said to me as he placed his chocolate penis pops on the table.

I glanced over, noting he'd arranged them like a bouquet on a florist's ball and had wrapped the handle in red silk. It did look pretty… if you didn't register that they were, in fact, penis replicas.

"I'll take that bet," Boho Lady said, her hands on her hips as she studied the table.

He glanced over at her perfectly sculpted male torso cake and gulped. "Make it ten."

She laughed. "You're on."

I held up my hands, indicating I was out of the betting, and inched toward Bootlegger, determined not to let him out of my sight.

"Time!" Maggie called. "Hands off your desserts!"

The six of us took a step back from the table. I glanced at my cupcakes and winced. The dip in the center had only gotten worse, and now instead of cute bikini tops and bottoms, they looked like I'd intentionally made saggy boobs with matching wedgies. Yikes.

"Better luck next time," Boho Lady said, sympathy in her tone.

I shrugged. It didn't matter. Not really. Any publicity was good publicity, right?

Maggie was busy showing off our creations to the spectators. I'd lost Julius among the crowd. But College Guy—Bootlegger—was just a few feet from me and had started to get fidgety. Ida May had disappeared as well. She'd probably depleted all her energy from yelling at Bootlegger. There was no telling when she'd be back.

College Guy shuffled from foot to foot, his eyes shifting back and forth as if paranoia had taken over. I placed a light hand on his arm.

He jumped, pulling away from me. "Don't."

I held my hands up in a surrender motion. "I'm here to help."

His eyes turned from brilliant green to ocean blue and he shook his head, fear and anxiety etched all over his face. College Guy had at least momentarily pushed aside Bootlegger. "You can't help with this."

"I can. We just need to—"

"Stop meddlin' in matters that are no concern to you, woman," College Guy's voice turned sharp and irritated as those eyes flickered back to green.

Bootlegger. He was back.

College Guy was fighting his presence and losing.

"Let him go," I said, my tone low and full of rage. "What you're doing is wrong."

"Wrong?" Bootlegger laughed. "Wait until you've been a ghost for over a hundred years. Then we'll see what you're willing to do to remember what a woman feels like under ye."

I gave him a flat stare.

His lips turned up into a twisted smile. "You look like the type."

Holy hell.

His eyes flashed blue again, and he took a step back, shaking his head. "I didn't... I mean I wouldn't..." He stared at me, confusion making his mouth work, but the words weren't coming. How could they? No one expected to be hijacked by a ghost pirate.

"You're okay," I said reassuringly, reaching out once more. This time he let me, and when my fingers brushed his arm, a small tremor ran through him. His eyes closed and he took a slow, steadying breath.

Leaning in, he lowered his voice. "What's happening to me?"

The fear and uncertainty in the young man's tone made anger surge through me. Bootlegger had to go. Now.

Lily's words rang in my head. *You don't need Julius.*

Would he even know a spell off the top of his head to expel a ghost? He might. I glanced back to where I'd last seen him, but he was still missing. Where had he gone? I had no idea, but I couldn't worry about it right then. The crowd was too thick and wound up for me to go look for him, and leaving College Guy was out of the question.

"Number four, Romance Between the Covers by Sunshine Fable!" Maggie was saying as she waved at Boho Lady. The crowd cheered and whistled, showing her their approval.

"What's your name?" I asked College Guy.

"Cal," he said and glanced over at Scarlett, frowning. "Do I know her?"

I shook my head. "Not that I'm aware of."

"But she… uh…" He held up a plastic room key. "I think I'm supposed to be meeting her later."

I sighed. Talk about forward. Chances were Scarlett didn't know his name either. "That's entirely up to you if you want to take her up on that offer, but I want to make sure it's you who's really making that decision."

"Huh?" His fingers tightened around the plastic keycard as he watched her, but then suddenly he shoved the key in his back pocket and whipped around, bringing his face inches from mine. "Stay out of it, *medium*."

I glared into Bootlegger's green eyes. "Not a chance."

He jerked back and gave me a sinister smile as he reached for Scarlett. She was busy waving to the crowd, too distracted to notice. But before he could snake his arm around her waist, I stepped between them and ignored the revulsion coursing through me as I grabbed his cheeks and kissed him.

Well, more like covered his lips with mine and breathed in his air.

All the noise, the crowd, the milling of people around us faded away. Static filled my ears and shifted to a low, buzzing noise.

Then I heard Bootlegger clear as day. "Nooooo! You'll pay for this, you meddlin' fool."

Cal's mouth was frozen into an O, his lips unmoving, thank goodness. The last thing I needed was for him to get the wrong idea and start kissing me.

Ice-cold air filled my mouth and lungs as I forcefully removed the ghost from Cal. My head swam as I swayed on my feet. I couldn't see. A pale grayness clouded my vision. There was nothing but cold.

Let him go, the faint sound of Lily's voice echoed deep in my mind.

Disoriented, I stilled and blinked, trying to peer through the fog.

Release him! Lily's voice was stronger now, demanding.

I dropped my hands and stepped back. My vision cleared, but I was still frozen to the bone and shivering. Anger and hatred coursed through my veins, and a low growl rumbled from deep in my throat.

Cal stood in front of me, his eyes wide and skin pale. "What did you do?" he asked, his tone shaky.

Unable to speak, I shook my head, clutching at my arms. My fingernails dug into my skin, biting so hard I wondered if I'd draw blood.

Pyper! Lily's unusually angry voice rang in my head. *What are you doing?*

I had no idea how to answer her. The rage storming inside me made me want to crawl right out of my skin. Nothing else mattered. I opened my mouth and screamed.

Chapter 10

AN INHUMAN SOUND came from me, ringing in my ears. It was so loud it drowned out all the voices and music from the after-hours chocolate party that was still in full swing. But I didn't care. The ice freezing my lungs started to melt, and my blood heated my skin as I fell to my knees, expelling everything I had, forcing the ghost from my lips.

Gray smoke swirled in front of me, rolling and turning, forming incoherent shapes until finally I was spent, silent, all the rage and frustration cast out, right along with Bootlegger.

The ghost solidified and stood right in front of me, his green eyes blazing with hatred. "You'll pay for this, *medium*."

Then with a loud pop, he vanished.

I slumped to the side, gasping in air, too weak to stand on my own. Holy cowbells. Is that what it was like for Jade and Julius when they were wielding spells? I shook my head. I hadn't used magic, just sheer will. But it cost me. My eyelids were heavy, and moving my limbs felt like wading through quicksand.

"Oh, honey." Boho Lady knelt down and offered me a hand. "It was only a silly competition. So you came in fourth. At least you beat Penis Pop Guy."

I stared up at her, my brows pinched. Was she serious? For the love of… I just nodded. Was it better for her to think I'd lost my mind over a competition? Probably. Explaining to a stranger that I'd just exorcised a ghost from Cal probably wouldn't go over too well.

"I… uh, just tripped. Can you help me up?" I lifted my heavy arm out to her.

She raised one skeptical eyebrow. "Tripped? With a scream like that, you'd think someone had ripped your heart out."

Glancing around at the unconcerned crowd, I wondered exactly how loud I'd actually been.

"Here, let's get you up." Boho Lady finally took my hand and hauled me to my feet with surprising strength.

"Did I make a fool of myself?" I asked, clutching the nearest table.

She shook her head. "No, you were mostly blocked by Penis Pop Guy. And the crowd was too busy cheering for the winner to notice you." She waved an impatient hand at Scarlett, who was obnoxiously posing for pictures and waving at the group of guys Cal had come in with.

Cal was standing off to the side of her, shifting from foot to foot as he stared at me, no doubt wondering if I'd lost my freakin' mind.

I must've started screaming right after the announcement was made, otherwise there was no way I'd have gone unnoticed. That was something at least. "I need to get out of here."

"This way." Boho Lady pointed me toward a side exit. "That leads out to the pool area. If you hurry, you can get out of here before the reporter is done with Scarlett. They usually interview all the contestants for their shipboard newsletter.

Judging by your pale face and shaking limbs, I'm guessing that's out of the question."

I held one hand out, noting the small tremors still shooting through me. Yikes. Yeah, time to go. I nodded. "Thanks."

She helped me to the exit, held the door open, and then waved. "Get some sugar in your system. It'll help."

I choked out a huff of laughter as the door closed softly behind me. All that time in the chocolate bar, and I hadn't tasted one darn thing. Didn't that just suck donkey butt.

I stared across the deck at the pool, the same one Jade and I had been swimming in earlier. The one we'd been in when I'd witnessed the murder of Vienna Vox. Damn, that had seemed like ages ago. Days even. Had it really only been five hours?

The wind of the Gulf picked up, chilling me. I wrapped my arms around myself and moved toward the entrance that led back to our stateroom. Would Julius be waiting for me? Or was he still in the ballroom? The thought of going back inside to face the party made bile rise in the back of my throat. I was done. Completely done with people—and ghosts for that matter. If I didn't get some rest, I was going to collapse.

I slipped through the heavy door back into the ship's interior. When I was halfway down the hallway, I stopped dead in my tracks and let out a small, startled gasp. Cal had appeared from an adjoining hallway right in front of me.

"Whoa," he said softly, grasping my upper arms lightly to keep me steady on my feet.

I glanced down at his hands and then back at him, raising both eyebrows.

"Sorry." He let go instantly. "You just looked a little unsteady there for a minute. I didn't want you to fall. Helping was the least I could do after what you did for me back there."

"I didn't do anything," I mumbled, wondering what exactly it was he thought I did.

He let out a snort. "No? Because it seems to me that *something* happened. And whatever you did fixed it."

"I…" I let out a sigh. He deserved to know he'd been possessed, didn't he? What if Bootlegger came back? What if he tried it again? "You're right. Something did happen."

He leaned a shoulder against the wall, waiting.

"I don't know where to start." I bit my bottom lip, hating that I sounded so unsure of myself. That wasn't me. I was a straight shooter. Always telling it like it was. But when it came to ghosts and the supernatural, one never knew how people were going to take things.

"How about you explain to me why I didn't have control over my actions." His face was troubled. "One minute I was having fun with my buddies, drinking a little rum, and the next…" He scrubbed his hand down his face. "The next I had my tongue down that woman's throat, but I swear on my mother it felt as if I was possessed or something. Jeesum. I have a girlfriend. A fiancée actually, just as soon as I get around to asking her. I was waiting until we got to Jamaica. Sunset proposal. The works. But now…"

Oh goodness. My heart sank. "Your girlfriend… was she in the audience?"

He nodded and averted his eyes.

"Cal?" I placed a light hand on his arm.

He all but flinched as he took a step back, putting distance between us.

I grimaced. "Sorry. I didn't mean anything by it. I'm not

Scarlett. I'm spoken for too."

"It's not that. Well, maybe it is. I just would hate for her to come find me talking to you and get the wrong idea. I mean, I know we weren't kissing, but I can't be sure what it would look like to her. And even if she did believe me about you, I sure as hell *was* kissing that other woman. But…" He paused, staring over my shoulder.

I glanced back. The hallway was empty. Thank goodness. "You weren't kissing her at all," I supplied, deciding he should know the truth no matter how fantastic it might seem to him. If his girl was going to dump his butt, he at least deserved to not have to carry the guilt that was so clearly swimming in his blue gaze.

"No?" He let out choked laughter. "I don't know who you were looking at, but it couldn't have been me. I can still taste the chocolate from her lips."

I shook my head. "No. What I mean to say is that you were kissing her against your will. Or at least you didn't have the control to say yes or no."

"I don't—"

"Hold on." I stared into his eyes, holding his gaze. "Right after you downed the rum, did you have the feeling that you were present but that your brain wasn't communicating with the rest of your body? Like you were just a visitor, forced to watch from the sidelines while someone else called the shots?"

He sucked in a breath. "Sort of."

I nodded. "That's because someone else had possession of your body."

"Possession?" His face crumpled with confusion, then almost instantly morphed into skepticism. "Is this some sort of joke? Are you seriously standing here, telling me I was possessed?"

Crap. He was a nonbeliever. Well, it hardly mattered now. He was going to get the truth whether he liked it or not. What he did with it was his business. No one was likely to lock me up for making up ghost stories, were they? Not anyone on this ship, not after Julius had been called in to take care of paranormal activity in one of the staterooms.

"Listen. I'm a medium. Do you know what that means?"

His eyebrows rose in surprise, then the corner of his mouth twitched into a tiny smile. "You pretend to hear people's dead relatives and give them false hope?"

"Cute." I narrowed my eyes at him. "No, I don't pretend to see anyone or give anyone false hope. But I do see and hear ghosts every once in a while."

"You're saying there was a ghost here tonight? And that ghost possessed me?" The mocking was gone now, replaced by a hint of curiosity. Maybe there was hope for him.

"Yes. Actually there were two ghosts in there. Ida May, the one who thinks we're BFFs. She followed me on the cruise and is mostly harmless. The other one though, Bootlegger. I believe he's tied to the ship."

"Bootlegger." Cal said the word as if he was talking to himself and frowned in concentration.

"Yeah. He was swimming in the rum when you drank it and decided to take your body for a spin. He kissed Scarlett… uh, the brunette in the red dress. Not you."

He crossed his hands over his chest and stared down at me. "And where do you come in? What was that when you… you know, sort of kissed me."

My head was starting to pulse, and I rubbed my temple above my left eye. "I didn't kiss you. I sucked Bootlegger out of your body."

His eyes widened. "Into yours? That sounds disturbing."

"No. I mean, he was there momentarily, and that's why I ended up screaming. That dispelled him."

"That's good. Except where is this ghost now?" He glanced over his shoulder as if searching for the body invader.

I shrugged. "No idea. He used too much energy. Depending on how strong he is, he'll be back sooner or later."

"And can he do that again? Should I be wary of drinking or eating anything else? Should I tell my friends?"

All good questions. And I didn't have an answer to any of them. "Honestly, I don't know. If I were you, I'd stick to unopened bottled beverages for now. At least until I can see about making sure he can't possess anyone else."

Cal crossed his arms over his chest. "Can you really do that?"

"I hope so." Then I gestured down the hallway at a tall, slim blonde who was headed right for him, her fists clenched and her jaw out. "I think you have company."

He spun. "Beth! There you are."

Beth shifted her gaze to me and scowled.

"Sorry," I whispered to him as I moved past him. When I got to Beth, I added, "Go easy on him. He's had a rough night."

She stopped dead in her tracks and gaped at me.

"I'm in room 1008. Come find me if you have questions." I didn't know why I added that last bit. Maybe because I was sure she was going to think he was lying his ass off. And the thought of him losing the woman he wanted to marry because some ghost decided to use Cal's body as his personal playground was too revolting. Bootlegger had already violated Cal's body. I wasn't going to stand by and let the ghost shatter his heart too.

Beth just stared at me with her mouth open as I passed her. I couldn't blame her. After the night she'd had, I'd probably gape at a crazy person too.

Some of my strength had returned to my limbs, but not much. Fatigue weighed me down, and instead of heading back into the ballroom to look for Julius, I sent him a quick text and pointed myself toward our room.

But just as I rounded the corner of the corridor leading to the staterooms, I stopped dead in my tracks.

Vienna Vox stood just inside an open elevator, longing and pain mixing in her dark, haunted eyes as she reached out to the man in front of her.

The man who happened to be my Julius.

Chapter 11

"Julius?" I whispered, not wanting to disturb any connection he might have with the ghost.

But he didn't hear me. Or if he did, he didn't acknowledge me.

Tears streamed down Vienna's sweet face as her lips curled into a sad, almost wistful smile. Who did she think he was? Had they known each other?

I pressed a hand to my stomach, trying to dispel the sinking feeling in my gut. Julius hadn't lived during her time, but they could've met as ghosts. At least I assumed they could have.

"Vivi," Julius said, his voice choked as his fingers reached hers. The pair clasped hands, their knuckles going white as they held on tight, both staring at the connection.

Magic crackled around them, and a burst of light nearly blinded me. I squinted, unsure of what I was seeing.

Then I let out an audible gasp and ran forward, reaching for Julius. He was pouring power into Vienna, both hands outstretched, magic crackling from his fingertips and straight into her chest. She had her head thrown back, her arms spread wide as she welcomed the magic. Magic that was filling her, turning her more solid.

"Julius!" I cried. "Stop!"

What was he doing? Trying to bring her back from the dead?

But he didn't falter. His focus was one hundred percent on the rock star ghost. Her head tilted up at the sound of my voice. Our eyes met and something stirred there. Recognition?

"Vienna?" I asked.

Her gaze tracked me as I moved forward.

"Do you know who killed you? Who threw you over the railing of the ship?"

She nodded once, her gaze shifting back to Julius.

This was good. His magic was fortifying her, helping her to stay coherent. Was he strong enough to bring her back to our world? Free her from her limbo? I prayed that was the case. "Who was it?"

Her eyes narrowed, then widened as she pointed in Julius's direction.

"What?" That couldn't be true. Julius had been a ghost when she'd been killed. And he'd been trapped in a hotel on Bourbon Street. "Are you sure?"

Her lips turned down into a nasty snarl as her dark eyes turned almost feral. She nodded once, and before I could ask her anything else, the elevator dinged and the doors started to close.

"Vienna!" Julius and I cried at the same time. But it was too late. The door cut off Julius's magic, and once again Vienna was gone.

Julius dropped to the floor as the brilliant light of his magic vanished. Behind us, the click of the door opening caught my attention. I spun, spotting a man in a maintenance uniform disappearing into the other room, the door slamming closed behind him. The sound echoed in the otherwise silent corridor.

Holy balls. How long had he been there? I had a moment of wondering what management would say if he brought his story to them. Or if he didn't, who was he and why was he ambivalent about massive amounts of magic flying around the interior of the ship?

I shook my head, putting the distraction out of my mind. None of that was my concern. "Julius?" I asked, giving him my full attention.

He turned to me, recognition dawning in his eyes as his gaze landed on me. "Pyper."

Pale and slightly out of breath, he held his arm out to me and I gladly went to him, wrapping both arms around his waist as he tucked me against his side. "What happened?" I asked him. "Where did Vienna come from?"

He shook his head. "Vienna?"

"Yeah. The ghost that was just here."

He frowned at me. "Ghost? I thought you were trying to keep Bootlegger from possessing anyone."

"I did. But you'd already left." Warning bells went off in my head. Something was way off. He'd left the ballroom early and now he seemed to have no memory of what just happened with Vienna. Maybe the magic had zapped his brain. "Are you all right?"

His arm tightened around me as he shook his head again. "Can we just go back to the room?"

"Sure." Exhaustion was taking over, and my eyes started to water. It had to be well past one in the morning, and I'd been up since before five. Not to mention, booting Bootlegger had drained me.

We kept ahold of each other as we walked in silence back to the room. And when I saw the number 1008 come into view, I nearly cried with relief. The day had started with such promise. We'd finally had our first date, or at least tried before we ended up on the House of Horrors cruise.

Julius opened the door for me, and the moment I slipped in, I headed for the bathroom, wasting no time getting ready for bed. But instead of choosing my black lace nightie, I pulled on pajama pants and a T-shirt. Our first time was not going to be right after I'd had to sort of kiss a college kid and then suck out Bootlegger's essence. Just no.

All I wanted to do was climb into bed and rest my head on Julius's chest.

When I exited the bathroom, my face scrubbed and my hair tied back, Julius's face broke out into a slow smile. "So, this is how you seduce your man?"

I laughed. "Yes. Soap in place of perfume and cotton jammies. Every man's dream. Don't you read *Cosmo*?"

Chuckling, he disappeared into the bathroom. By the time he reemerged, shirtless and in sleep shorts, I was already snuggled up in bed, facing the sliding glass door. The moon shone down, bouncing off the dark water, and all I could think about was Vienna and her scream as she plunged to her death.

I let out an involuntary shudder.

Julius slid into the bed and wrapped his arms around me, pulling me close. "What is it, Pyper?" he whispered.

He was so warm, his body a comfort pressed against mine. I shook my head. "Nothing. I was just seeing Vienna go over the railing. Even though I know it happened years ago, it didn't feel that way to me. It was like I was right there, watching her life come to an end."

He pressed his lips to my temple, kissing me gently as he trailed his fingers up and down my bare arm. "I can imagine."

I was sure he could. One doesn't exist as a ghost for over a hundred years and not see some crazy crap go down. "If we figure out who her killer was, do you think it will free her from reliving her death?"

His hand stilled. "Probably. But only if you can reach her long enough to give her answers. You haven't actually been able to communicate with her, have you?"

I turned over on my back and stared up at him. "No, not really. Nothing beyond an acknowledgement that she could see me. But I thought you had."

His brows furrowed together. "No. What made you think that?"

"Back at the elevators. She was focused on you, while you… What were you doing? All that magic, it sort of looked like you were trying to—" I clamped my mouth closed and shook my head again. "I don't know what you were trying to do, but Vienna looked solid and coherent like your magic was grounding her or something."

Julius pushed himself up on his elbow and gazed down at me for a second before sitting all the way up and running a hand through his dark hair.

I mimicked his movement and pulled the blanket up, covering myself. It was stupid, really. I was fully clothed and had nothing to hide, not that I ever worried about that anyway, but in the darkness after such a draining night, I couldn't help but feel exposed. "What is it?"

He stared straight ahead, focusing on nothing. "I don't remember."

I let out the breath I'd been holding. "I was afraid of that."

"The magic. Vienna. How I got to the elevator." He turned his head and stared me straight in the eye. "I don't remember leaving the ballroom."

A flicker of fear flittered through me. "You're saying you blacked out?"

He nodded. "I guess so. Or… disappeared."

The hollowness in his tone made my heart sink. When Julius had been a ghost, he'd been able to show up in solid form for short periods of time, then he'd just disappear. That hadn't happened since Bea had worked a spell to turn him permanently human. It didn't make sense it would happen now. Unless her spell was backfiring. But he was here, solid as could be, and I refused to entertain that line of thought. I reached for his hand, gently taking it in both of mine. "You didn't disappear."

"How do you know? Were you with me?"

I shook my head. "You know I wasn't. I was on that stage dealing with Bootlegger."

His hand tightened on mine. "How did that go?"

A small shudder accompanied the memory of sucking Bootlegger from Cal as if I were a succubus, but I ignored it. "It went. I'm fine. So is everyone else. I'll tell you about it later. Right now I'd rather talk about what happened with you. You're shaken."

He let out a long breath. "It's disarming that you can read me so well."

I gave him a small smile. "Better that than a clueless girlfriend."

That got a chuckle out of him. But he sobered instantly. "I don't know what happened. One minute I was in the ballroom, watching you, but then I heard something. Or someone. A voice calling to me. So I turned around, spotted Vienna Vox in the doorway, and then... nothing."

"You don't remember leaving?" I'd seen him moving toward the doors. The crowd had been rowdy, a little out of control, and Julius had been the one person not enjoying the party. At least now I knew why.

"No. I saw her and then the next thing I knew, I heard you calling my name, the electric remnants of magic clinging to my fingers."

"Holy crap. That's... unnerving."

He got out of the bed and started pacing the small room. "It's worse than that."

"How?"

Stopping, he gritted his teeth, then said, "I was lost. Blank. How do I know I didn't just fade out again? Like I used to before Bea did whatever she did to bring me back from the shadows?"

My heart sped up at his words. He feared the same thing I did. "You think Bea's spell is fading?"

He raised his hands. "I have no idea. I can't remember anything."

I climbed out of bed, desperate to touch him. To reassure myself he was whole, even though the fact that he was solid was as clear as day. But when I reached out for him, he shook his head and took a small step back.

Disappointment exploded in my chest. He was pushing me away. Just like last time things got hard. "Don't do this, Julius,"

I said softly. "A week ago, you promised me you wouldn't run again."

"Last week I thought I was here to stay."

Here. He meant here as in on Earth as a flesh-and-blood man. Not one who faded in and out of my life. "But you are here to stay. I saw you. I saw you leaving the ballroom and I saw you with Vienna. I don't know what happened in between, but you were here. And you were powerful. The magic you were wielding…" I sucked in a breath, remembering the fantastic light illuminating the both of them. "The magic was powerful. Intense. Not something a ghost could do. So you may not remember. We can work through that. Maybe you wielded too much magic and it caused temporary memory loss, but you were here. And when Vienna vanished, you didn't."

He averted his eyes, appearing to process my words. Then he bowed his head in my direction. "Thank you."

This time when I took a step, reaching for him, he pulled me close, giving me a fierce hug.

"There's nothing to thank me for," I said, my voice muffled against his bare chest.

He kissed me on the top of my head. "There's plenty. But for now I'm thankful just to be holding you."

I let out a sigh as my bones melted. *Thankful to be holding me.* No man had ever whispered such tender, intimate words to me before. Never been so honest and vulnerable before. Never made me feel *cherished* before. Tears stung the back of my eyes as raw emotion welled up from the depths of my soul. But I blinked them back and pulled away, staring up into his deep green eyes. "I'm thankful for that too."

His lips curved into a whisper of a smile. Then he pulled

away, and keeping his hand wrapped around mine, he tugged me back to bed. "Come on, my beautiful one. It's been a long day. Let's get some sleep."

I waited for him to climb back into the bed, then followed. He lay on his back, arms open to me. I snuggled in next to him with my head on his shoulder. And when his arms came around me, holding me tight, warmth filled all the empty crevices of my heart and soul.

He was my one. I was sure of it.

I only hoped he felt the same.

Chapter 12

"Late night?" Jade asked with a knowing smile. We were in the main dining hall having breakfast. I'd been doing my best to tune out the din of the other diners as they scraped their utensils against the china and planned their days. All I wanted to do was sleep.

I covered my mouth as I yawned. My eyes watered, and although it was only ten in the morning, I was already contemplating a nap. "Yep, but you can stop looking at me like that. Nothing happened."

Kane moved his hand to Jade's knee and whispered something to her that made her blush.

"At least nothing happened in our room. You two on the other hand… Looks like you both are rather, um, satisfied."

Jade's face turned scarlet as Kane chuckled.

I shook my head at her and let out a laugh of my own. "Damn, Jade. You're married. And trying to start a family. I don't think you need to be embarrassed about having the sex."

"I'm not," she quipped as she straightened her shoulders. "I'm just remembering."

Oh man. Not the conversation I needed to be having with my best friend's wife. "Kane?"

"Hmm?" He finally tore his eyes from Jade and glanced at me.

"Cut it out."

He frowned. "I'm not doing anything."

"Right. I can see your hand drifting up her skirt from here. It's not exactly what I need to see at breakfast. You know?" Especially since Julius had been gone before I'd even woken up. He'd hadn't even left a note, and I still hadn't seen or heard from him this morning. Which meant I was the third wheel.

Kane cleared his throat and put his hands on the table where they could be seen. But the disappointed look on Jade's face had me rolling my eyes.

"You guys are either adorable or gross. I can't decide."

"Adorable," they both said at the same time.

I pushed the eggs around my plate and silently agreed. They were perfect for each other. I'd known it almost instantly. At least from Kane's end. I'd never seen him fall for someone so quickly. And Jade, she was strong, didn't put up with his bull, and understood him in ways no one else could. He was a demon hunter, and she was a white witch. They spent more time fighting the evil forces of New Orleans than they did anything else. Who else would put up with that kind of life disruption?

"Do you want to join me at the spa today?" Jade asked, pushing her plate away. "Or do you have plans with Julius?"

I glanced up at her, suddenly aware I'd been staring at the same lump of eggs for who knew how long. "Spa? That sounds wonderful. But I should probably find Julius first and make sure we don't have other plans." Not that he seemed to be worried about what I was doing. Still, I would be unsettled until I talked to him.

"He's right there." Kane pointed over my shoulder.

I spun, finding a freshly showered and shaved Julius sitting at a table with Muse, the sexy rocker. Frowning, I stared at them. He was animated, talking with his hands as she threw back her head and laughed. Seriously? He'd left without waking me up, and now he was sitting at a table with Muse, cracking jokes while ignoring that I was less than twenty feet away?

Why was I on this trip again? Because I could've done without the body-snatcher escapade the night before.

I saw Muse slide a piece of paper over to Julius right before she stood up.

He tucked the small folded-up note into his front pocket and leaned back in the chair, legs stretched out as he watched her go. And I really do mean watched her go. His gaze followed her all the way to the double doors, only breaking when she disappeared from view.

"Ass," I muttered. But I'd miscalculated and his head jerked up.

His frown turned to a grimace.

That was quite enough. Stalking over to him, I placed my hands on my hips. "Having fun?"

He stood. "Good morning."

I raised one eyebrow. "Is it? It's not quite how I'd pictured this would go." I hadn't woken up in his arms, hadn't had breakfast in bed, and I'd completely missed the glorious sunrise over the Gulf. And lazy morning lovemaking? Nowhere on the horizon at this point.

He moved to stand in front of me, his expression apologetic. "I'm sorry, Pyper." He tucked a lock of my hair behind my ear, and I jerked back.

"Sorry for what exactly? Flirting with Muse? Or disappearing this morning without leaving a note? After last night, a person could've been worried about you."

Although he'd stiffened when I'd rejected his touch, one side of his mouth twitched up as my voice trailed off. His eyes softened as he gazed down at me. "You were worried?"

Frustration took over, and I slammed my hand against his chest, pushing him back. "Yes, I was worried, you idiot. You couldn't remember last night after the incident with Vienna. Then this morning your side of the bed was empty and didn't even look disturbed."

He let out a soft chuckle and moved in closer as he covered my hand with his. "I didn't sleep on my side. I slept on yours."

The softness in his tone combined with the glint in his eyes deflated my anger, and I let out a breath. "You could've woken me up, you know."

"I should have." He bent and brushed his lips over my cheek. "Hell, I wanted to. But you were sleeping so soundly I didn't want to disturb you."

My pulse started to quicken. "And a note?"

"Didn't even occur to me as I was trying to make as little noise as possible. It was before dawn."

I pulled back and stared up at him. "Before dawn? Did you sleep at all?"

"A bit. Mostly I just held you."

My heart melted and the anger finally dissipated. Who could resist that? But then I remembered him sitting with Muse and the note she'd passed him. "Care to tell me what you've been up to since before dawn?" Crap. That sounded more like an accusation than a question.

"Thinking mostly." He tilted his head toward an empty table, and when I didn't resist, he tugged me over and pulled out a chair for me.

Gentlemanly. That was Julius. Considerate and kind. Usually. "Thanks."

He took his seat and waved over a waitress. After ordering a black coffee, he turned to me. "Want something?"

I ordered a double mocha latte and a chocolate muffin. Ever since last night, I'd been craving chocolate something fierce. When she left us alone, I gave Julius my full attention. "So…?"

"So," he echoed. "I couldn't sleep, and I was restless. Agitated, really, after blacking out a portion of the night before. And instead of waking you, I decided it was best to go to the gym. I did a lot of sit-ups and push-ups, then moved on to the treadmill. By the time I got back, you were already gone."

Sit-ups. My gaze dropped, imagining what was hiding under his cotton shirt. I'd seen him shirtless just the night before, and those abs… Wow. My fingers twitched to be touching him right then and there.

"Pyper?" he asked.

I jerked my eyes back up, meeting his gaze. "Yeah?"

He gave me a knowing smile, having had no trouble figuring out what I'd been thinking. "Perhaps you'd like to join me next time. Hold my legs while I do my reps?"

My mouth went dry thinking about touching him. Holy hell. What was wrong with me? My hormones were raging like an eighteen-year-old's. I cleared my throat. "As enticing as that offer may be, I suspect you don't really need my help."

"It's not a matter of need," he said, his voice suddenly throaty.

I gave him a slow smile and leaned forward. "I think the next time I see your abs, I'd like a little privacy."

His eyes smoldered as he gazed at me.

Everything heated, and I wondered what he would do if I asked him to take me back to the room without waiting for our food. But just then the waitress arrived with our coffees and my muffin. The rich aroma of the coffee reached my senses and I let out a sigh, deciding if I couldn't have Julius right then, then the mocha latte and the muffin were close second choices.

The warm chocolate muffin melted on my tongue, and I closed my eyes, letting out a small moan of pleasure, lost in my little moment of ecstasy.

And when I opened my eyes, Julius's intense gaze made me flush.

Leaning in, he said, "Do that again."

I swallowed thickly. "Do what?" Flush? Because I was pretty certain my face was already resembling a ripe tomato.

"Make that sound. It drives me a little bit insane."

My insides started to tingle. But as much as I wanted to devour the muffin, to give him what he wanted, I pushed it away. "Not until you tell me why you were having breakfast with Muse."

All the heat and sexual tension drained from his face as he sat back, cupping his coffee mug. "Right." He took a breath. "What little sleep I got last night was dream-ridden. Unsettling dreams about Vienna Vox's death. Not what you saw, her being thrown over the ship railing, but fear she was going to die in all kinds of horrible ways. Like I knew her death was coming, but couldn't do anything to stop it." He shrugged. "I suppose it's because I interacted with her last night, and it may mean nothing, but for some reason I can't shake the feeling that she *knew* she was going to die before it happened."

As horrible as that was, it wasn't necessarily a surprise. If she'd been stalked and harassed long enough, it would've been a fear she lived with. "And Muse? What does she have to do with this?"

He flattened his hands out on the table. "She was part of the band back then. I wanted to hear her take on what happened."

"You asked her about Vienna's death, and that turned to flirting and laughing?" Even though I didn't believe for one minute Julius was interested in the rocker, though she *was* sexy when she wasn't falling-down drunk, it was hard to believe one would find humor when speaking about a friend's death.

"She didn't want to talk about Vienna past the basics that we already know. But she did want to flirt and tell me all about the upcoming tour her band has signed on for. Forty cities in forty days. Starting in New Orleans when we get back." He reached into his pocket and produced the note she'd given him. It had a phone number and the name Jack Jackson. "This is who I call for VIP tickets if I want backstage passes to hang out with the band."

I eyed the number, ire and full-on girl rage flaming to life in my chest. "She invited you, just you, to hang backstage with the band?"

He crumpled up the paper and pushed it to the side of the table. "I have no intention of indulging her."

That was what I liked to hear. A small smile tugged at my lips and I started to feel like a bit of an idiot for being jealous. Julius had never done anything to make me think he was interested in anyone else. I snagged the paper and stuffed it in my pocket. "Just in case we need access to her at some point."

He studied me for a moment, then nodded as his shoulders relaxed. "I always did like smart women."

Damn. "Flirting will get you everywhere."

He chuckled. "I can hardly wait." That urge to tug him to our room came roaring back, but he pushed the muffin toward me and said, "Now finish your breakfast so I can hear that sexy little noise you make."

Heat shot from my belly to my nether regions. Hell. What had I started with that muffin? Something delicious that had nothing to do with chocolate. Holding his gaze, I bit once again into the still-warm muffin, and without conscious thought, another tiny moan escaped from my lips. Cripes. The muffin and whatever they put in it should be illegal.

His eyes glinted and the hungry look on his face had me swallowing hard.

I stood, grabbing the muffin with one hand and holding the other out to Julius. "We need to go. What I have planned requires privacy."

He didn't hesitate, and the next thing I knew, it was Julius who was tugging me back to our room.

Chapter 13

THE ELEVATOR DOORS shut, and as soon as we started to descend, Julius reached over and slid his hand into mine. His thumb traced small circles over the inside of my wrist, sending a ripple of pleasure through me.

The gentleness of his touch always had a way of making me feel treasured, something I hadn't had much experience with. At least not with a significant other. My mother had her moments, and I knew Kane would do anything for me. But this was different. Special.

I glanced down at our connected hands, watching him trace those little circles. The small gesture was more intimate than anything in recent memory. And suddenly, despite the innuendo and the flirting at breakfast, I was nervous.

And vulnerable.

Once we took the next step, we wouldn't be able to erase it. We'd either be closer, or everything would go to hell. I wasn't sure if I was ready for that.

But when the elevator doors opened and Julius wrapped his arm around my shoulder, pulling me close, I knew I was a goner. He smelled of sunshine and faint, manly musk.

Heaven

Neither of us were in a hurry now as we took our time working our way to the room.

"Julius?" I asked, my head tilted up.

He glanced down, his eyes soft. "Hmm?"

I wasn't even sure what I wanted to say. All I knew was that I wanted to be closer to this man. To connect with him on a deeper plane. Instead of answering, I pressed my palm to his cheek and rose up, brushing my lips over his. The kiss was brief, tender, and full of promise as his arms tightened around me.

He didn't move for a moment as he searched my eyes. Then he nodded and bent his head, covering my mouth with his.

I melted into him. He was warm and tasted faintly of sugar and coffee. The world faded away, leaving me wrapped up in the slow, intoxicating kiss that had my pulse racing. My fingers curled in his button-down shirt as he slid his hand to my hip, holding me there.

"I'm not sure I deserve you," Julius said, nuzzling my neck.

I let out a small startled laugh. "Deserve?"

"Yeah." He lifted his head and in a throaty voice said, "But I also don't think I give a damn if I don't."

My smile widened. "Thank the goddess for that. Because right now, the only one I want is you."

His hand tightened around mine, and without another word, he tugged me down the hall to our room. When we were finally inside, I stood at the end of the bed, waiting as he dropped the keycard on the small nightstand.

Of all the ways I'd imagined our first time together, it hadn't been at ten in the morning with me wearing a ponytail and cutoff jean shorts. I looked like a walking advertisement for some trendy apparel store, not a sexy temptress ready to seduce her man.

Why hadn't I thought to at least wear a sundress? Probably because I didn't own any. I had plenty of dresses, but they were on the sexy side, good for nightlife, not daywear. No, mostly I wore jeans, shorts, and tank tops.

At least I had a nice bra and panty set on. I always did. Black demicup lace with a rich red bow.

I crooked a finger at him, indicating I wanted him to come closer.

He didn't disappoint. In three swift steps, he was standing in front of me, one hand cupping my neck and the other brushing the bright-pink strip of my hair back. "You do things to me, Pyper."

My breath caught at the intensity in his tone. I swallowed and gave him my flirty smile. "Not yet, but I will."

Heat flashed in his eyes as he stared at my mouth.

I darted my tongue over my lower lip just to see his reaction.

His body tensed, and then without warning, he lifted me up and turned to sit on the edge of the bed with me on top of him, my legs wrapped around his waist. "Do that again," he said, his voice husky.

"Do what," I asked, totally distracted by the feel of his chest rippling beneath his shirt.

Running his fingers down my spine, he said, "I want to see you lick your lip again."

"Oh," I breathed, reveling in his touch and the small tingles of pleasure sparking through my body.

He had his gaze locked on my mouth as he waited.

I wondered how long he'd stare at me like that if I just

waited him out, but his other hand came up and brushed my cheek, and without even thinking about it, I wetted my lips in anticipation.

"Perfect. Utterly perfect," he whispered and leaned in, claiming me with a heated kiss. Burying my fingers into his thick hair, I sank into him, my body instantly coming alive. I wanted him. More than I'd ever wanted anyone.

But Julius seemed content to take his time. He had one hand on my thigh and the other on the back of my neck and neither were moving. But his lips were. He'd turned his attention to my neck and was working his way down to my shoulder.

"You're going to torture me, aren't you," I teased, sliding my hands down until I found the top button of his shirt.

He glanced up, an amused, wry grin in place. "Isn't that the goal?"

I chuckled. "I suppose so, just as long as there's a payoff in the end."

"Oh, there's gonna be a payoff. Or two."

"Two?" I raised both eyebrows, my smile widening.

"At least." He dipped his head again, and this time ghosted his lips over my rapidly beating pulse.

That was more than I could take, and I made quick work of the rest of his buttons. When I pressed my hands to his bare chest, he glanced down as if he hadn't realized what I'd been doing.

"This has to go," I whispered, pushing the shirt over his shoulders.

"Gladly." He stripped the garment off and twisted as he turned to toss it on the floor. And as he did, I caught sight of something I hadn't seen before on the back of his shoulder.

Running my fingers over the faint outline, I studied what appeared to be a dragon. "When did you start this?"

"Start what?" He glanced at his shoulder and stiffened. Then next thing I knew, he was picking me up and placing me on my feet as he stood.

"Julius?" I stood completely still, acutely aware something had just happened, but I had no idea what. "What's wrong?"

He twisted in front of the mirror and craned his neck. When he got a good look at the tattoo, he let out a low hiss. "Dammit!"

I moved to stand beside him.

He poked at his shoulder and back, stretching sideways in order to inspect the design. Then he dropped his hands, straightened, and stared himself in the eye.

After a few moments, I placed a soft hand on his forearm and asked, "Want to tell me what's happening here?"

He turned haunted eyes on me. "I've never gotten a tattoo."

I opened my mouth to protest, because clearly he did have one, but I closed it, understanding that he believed he'd never had one done. Frowning, I shifted to stand behind him, inspecting the faded outline. It wasn't fresh, so there was no way someone had inked it on him the night before while he'd been blacked out. That left memory loss or some sort of—what the hell? The tattoo started to darken, and then the scales started to shimmer silver.

I gasped and blinked rapidly, not believing my eyes.

"What?" Julius twisted again just in time to see the silver fade.

Our eyes met in the mirror and then, as if on cue, we both

said, "Magic."

✧　✧　✧

"SHE SAID SOMETHING about heading to the spa today," I said to Julius as we strode down the hallway toward Jade and Kane's room. "If she's not in her room, we can either wait her out, or I can go find her."

"We'll wait," Julius said.

I pressed my lips together in a thin line. Julius hadn't been able to pinpoint any specific spell that had been cast on him. All he could say was that ever since the night before, he'd been unsettled. Anxious. And short on patience. I'd been aware of the unsettled part, but he'd done a fine job of hiding the other two. Still, I wasn't nearly as content to sit around while Jade got her massage and her toes painted. Someone had spelled him.

It was really the only explanation for the tattoo. He hadn't had it last week. I knew. I'd spent a considerable amount of time admiring him while he'd been shirtless in my kitchen after a workout with Kane. A dragon that spanned three-quarters of his back didn't just appear out of nowhere. Nor did the silver scales that came and went, sometimes glowing and sometimes barely visible.

Glowing tattoos weren't something a girl missed. Especially when they were fire-breathing dragons.

If Jade wasn't in her room, it would take an act of Congress to keep me from tracking her down. Julius had been spelled. And he hadn't even realized it. That took serious skill. If it had happened the night before, there was another very powerful witch onboard.

A chill crawled up my spine.

I should've known the Witches' Council wouldn't have sent Julius on a simple mission. If it was just a matter of cleansing one room of a spell, they could've done that while the ship was in port. There was something much more sinister happening on the high seas.

Julius rapped three times on Jade's door. Heavy footsteps sounded from inside just before Kane swung the door open. He was disheveled, his shirt on inside out, and his hair was mussed as if he'd just gotten out of bed.

"Sorry to interrupt," I said as I moved past him, not waiting for an invitation.

"Sure, come right on in. Don't mind us," Kane muttered, running his hand over his head, trying to tame his dark locks.

The water was running in the bathroom and a light shone under the door. The rumpled bedcovers told me more than I cared to know.

"Sorry, man," Julius said. "We wouldn't be here if it wasn't important."

The irritation lining his face vanished. "What's going on?"

The bathroom door swung open and Jade hurried into the room, her cheeks flushed as she tightened the knot of her robe. Obviously Julius and I hadn't been the only ones taking advantage of the at-sea day by spending it in bed. Only they appeared to have had more success than we had.

Lucky bastards.

"What's wrong?" Jade asked, peering at me. "Your anxiety is off the charts."

I sighed. It was pointless to ask her to stop reading me. Not when I was this worked up. She could block emotions, but when someone close to her was upset, it was nearly impossible.

"Julius has been spelled," I blurted.

Jade spun to stare at him. "How?"

He shrugged. "No idea. But I bear the marks." Then he turned and stripped his shirt off.

I moved to stand next to Kane, leaving room for Jade to inspect the now almost invisible tattoo. The lines had all but vanished, but if I squinted, I could still make out the dragon shape.

"What in the world?" she said under her breath as she frowned. Then she raised her hand as if to touch him but paused and asked, "Do you mind?"

"Go ahead." Julius stood perfectly still and silent as she traced her fingers over the tattoo. But after a moment, her frown deepened.

"What makes you think this is a spell?" she asked.

Julius's brows furrowed. "It wasn't there before and I have no memory of getting a tattoo. What else could it be?"

Before she could answer, I added, "It changes in intensity as well. Earlier the scales were glowing silver and the outline was a lot more defined. This acts almost like an illusion."

Jade whipped her long strawberry-blond hair up into a haphazard bun and tilted her head as she continued to examine the tattoo. As we stood there, it all but faded from his skin. She blew out a breath. "This is very odd."

"That's one way of putting it," I said dryly.

Kane slipped his arm over my shoulders and squeezed my arm, a silent gesture of support.

"Do you mind if I use a little magic to see if I can get it to reappear?" Jade asked Julius. "I want to see if I can sense anything from it."

"Sense what?" I asked, confused. "You mean you want to see if whoever did it left some sort of energy behind?"

Jade nodded. "Exactly. Sometimes I can get traces from objects if it's fresh, especially when the piece is handmade. There's an emotional element there, you know?"

"Sure." I brushed a dark lock of hair out of my eyes. "But this isn't an object. It's Julius's skin."

"I know." Jade turned and gave me a small reassuring smile. "But it was done by hand. I just want to see if there was magic left behind in the ink. It should be easy enough to do."

"Go ahead," Julius said, straightening his shoulders. "A little magical probing isn't going to hurt anything."

"Famous last words," I mumbled.

Kane's grip on my shoulder tightened as he leaned down to whisper, "She'll be careful."

"I know," I whispered back, swallowing my rising fear. If he had been spelled, it could literally mean anything. Even some sort of black-magic curse. Not too long ago, Jade had been cursed herself. And the only way to reverse it was to find the witch—or in her case, the angel—who did it.

"Just relax," Jade soothed as she pressed her palm to the back of his shoulder. A faint outline of white light shimmered over her skin, making her glow like an ethereal being. Then the light spread over Julius's back, tracing the outline of the dragon, highlighting every scale, every curve of the creature's body, every flicker of flame shooting from its open mouth.

"Whoa." I couldn't tear my eyes away from the dragon that now covered his entire back and right arm. But instead of the silver scales I'd seen before, they were now brilliant orange and red with hints of yellow. Its talons were obsidian, and its eyes brilliant green. Had it been an actual tattoo, it was the type of work done by a master that would've taken multiple sittings.

Jade let out a tiny grunt of frustration. With her face scrunched up in concentration, her light brightened and took on a shimmering quality. "It's not working—" she started, but then suddenly her magic broke free of the dragon and spread over his entire body, lighting him up like a human Christmas tree. "There. Got it."

Her eyes closed and her frown deepened almost to a scowl.

Oh geez. Whatever she'd found was not good. Dread circled and crawled right into my heart.

"What is it, Jade?" Julius asked softly.

She dropped her hand and took a step back. Her magic vanished, leaving Julius standing in the shadows as he turned to face her. Jade turned to me, and the resigned expression on her face rooted me to the floor. "It's not magic. It's another soul."

Chapter 14

"WHAT?" JULIUS AND I said at the same time.

Jade ran a hand across her brow and sank down into a blue polyester armchair. "It's not a spell. But there is emotional energy there that isn't yours," she said to Julius. "And it's active."

"That can't be…" Julius turned to stare in the wall mirror.

Everything in me tensed at Jade's words as ice crawled up my spine. The memory of feeling like a stranger in my own body came roaring back, and I wrapped my arms around myself, my nails digging into my skin. Last year I'd found myself sharing my body with another soul. A magical one who'd been a medium. It was why I could see and talk to ghosts now. The extra soul I'd carried had been extracted and inserted into a woman who'd lost hers. It had been unusual to say the least. My parting gift had been the ability to speak with the dead.

"We have to get in touch with Lailah," I said, already reaching for my phone. Angels were soul guardians, and Lailah was one we knew we could trust. If anyone could help Julius, it was her. "Crap! No signal."

Jade glanced at hers and shook her head, indicating she was in the same boat, so to speak. "There is nothing she can do from

New Orleans right now anyway."

"How did this happen? Julius is a witch. He'd notice something like that, wouldn't he?" I asked Jade.

She bit down on her bottom lip. "I probably would, but only because of my empath abilities. But when you had another soul, you didn't know at first, right?"

"No, but—"

"It happened last night," Julius said, cutting me off. "When we were breaking the spell in room 1538."

Jade's eyes widened. "You knew?"

I sucked in a sharp breath. He knew he was carrying another soul and had still been willing to get naked with me? A surge of anger heated my face but dissipated as he shook his head.

"No. I didn't realize it until just now." He sat down on the couch, his elbows propped on his knees as he held his head in his hands.

I hurried across the room and sat next to him, placing my hand on his leg.

He flinched and jerked his head up as if I'd burned him.

"Whoa." I pulled my hand back. "Sorry. I didn't mean—"

"No." He shook his head, his eyes pinched with regret. "It's not you. As soon as Jade said I have another soul on board, her words registered as true, and now I can feel the foreign energy and it's making my skin crawl."

I stared at Jade, silently imploring her to do something. Anything. But deep down I knew she couldn't. Separating souls wasn't one of her talents. Only the angels could separate souls. And even then it wasn't guaranteed which soul remained in the body. The angels always chose the soul that would do the most good for their purposes. If we took Julius to them, they could very well decide to let him go and give his body to the invader. There was often nothing angelic about the angels who watched over our souls. Their world was very black and white.

She stood there, her head tilted to the side, a contemplative expression on her face.

Kane glanced from her to me. When our eyes met, his lips pressed into a thin grim line. "Jade?"

"Yeah?" she answered, still staring at Julius.

"What are you thinking?" he asked softly.

"There's something different about this. Different from when Pyper and the others had been compromised. I can't quite put my finger on it though."

Julius turned his attention to her. "What do you mean?"

My fingers ached with the urge to caress him, to soothe the tension lines around his temples. But I held still, waiting for Jade's explanation.

She sat on the bed, tucking one leg underneath her. "When this happened to Pyper, Kat, and Charlie, I didn't pick up on the second soul. Lailah tipped us off. I would've never known. But you"—she waved at Julius—"I can clearly distinguish the two souls. In the previous case it was as if only one soul could be in charge at once. What's happening here seems to be more of a partnership, more like a guest and less like a takeover."

"A guest?" I blurted, knowing all too well how awful and invasive it was to have someone make themselves at home in your body. "You've got to be joking. Julius didn't just open himself up to some random soul and welcome them with open arms."

"Of course he didn't," she said, frowning at me. "That's not what I meant."

Julius looked at me then, his expression resigned. Reaching for my hand, he tucked it between both of his. "It's okay, Pyper. She's only trying to help."

My righteous indignation fled and guilt streamed in. Jade was one of my best friends, but I was letting fear take over. Fear for what had happened to me in the past and fear for what this meant for Julius's future. The angels, despite their name, weren't to be trusted. They'd proved that one too many times while touting that their decisions were for the greater good. Except when they weren't. Like when the high angel made decisions to protect her secret son.

I squeezed Julius's fingers, comforted to be touching him again and then turned my attention to Jade. "I'm sorry. You know I didn't mean to lash out at you. I'm just frustrated."

"And worried," she said gently. "We all are." She turned to Kane. "I think we better stick close to them for the time being."

He nodded, a lock of dark hair falling over one eye.

A tiny bit of the pressure in my chest eased. They were the two most powerful people I knew. If anything went haywire, I wanted them in the mix.

Julius sat completely still with his gaze aimed straight ahead, his eyes slightly glazed.

"Hey…" I ran my hand up his arm.

He didn't move. He didn't even flinch like he had the time before.

"Julius?" I said, raising my voice.

He turned his head to me, a flicker of recognition registering in his gaze.

"There you are. Where'd you go?" My heart was thundering again. Checking out like that couldn't be a good sign.

Jade leaned forward, studying him. No doubt she was still reading him and the other soul, but she wasn't talking. Not yet.

"He's upset." Julius's voice seemed far away, as if we were hearing his words carried through an open window.

"He?" Jade asked.

Julius nodded. "He. But he's not communicating with me. I don't know if he even can. He's full of turmoil, and I'm pretty certain he's not going anywhere until whatever it is he's upset about is resolved."

"It has something to do with that room," I guessed. "You said it happened there. But why?"

Jade stood and started pacing. "I'm guessing he was trapped there somehow, and when we cleansed the room, he was freed but needed a vessel. Wielding magic can leave us vulnerable to outside sources because our defenses are down. My guess is that since Julius has a history with the other world, he was probably easier to infiltrate."

Not that Jade didn't have plenty of her own experiences, but Julius had been a ghost for almost a century before he'd been brought back from the dead. That kind of thing left a mark no matter how you sliced it.

"Okay." I stood. "So what do we do to get rid of the body snatcher?"

Julius shook his head, his lips curling into the faintest hint of a smile. The expression soothed the ache that had formed in my gut.

"That's a very good question—" Jade started.

But Julius cut her off. "He doesn't want to be here. With me, I mean. That much I can tell."

"How?" I asked.

He shrugged. "A feeling."

On impulse, I turned and said, "Let me try something. Remember what I told you about how Bootlegger invaded Cal last night and how I was able to extract him?"

Julius stared at me, then recognition lit his green eyes as he nodded.

"Let me at least try that. It certainly couldn't hurt."

Julius nodded, his expression contemplative. "You're right. It's worth a try."

I smiled and moved in as if I were going to kiss him.

But Jade spoke up, interrupting. "What are you talking about?"

Right. I hadn't exactly filled her in on all the details of the night before. Trying for a shortened version, I explained Bootlegger's goal, what happened with Cal, and how I'd extracted the ghost.

"So you're saying you can suck ghosts out of people?" There was awe in her tone.

"It appears so. At least it worked with Bootlegger."

"Whoa. That's interesting." Then she peered at Julius. "Do you think you're harboring a ghost? It would explain why your situation feels different than Pyper's, Kat's, and Charlie's. There was no ghost, just lost souls."

He shrugged. "I can't be sure, but it seems unlikely there was just a soul trapped in that room, right?"

"Yeah. It does." Jade stepped back, taking her place next to Kane. "All right. I'll be here in case anything goes haywire."

That was a small comfort. I still didn't have much of a handle on my new ability, and having her near, knowing how powerful she was, certainly helped me feel more at ease.

"Ready?" I asked Julius.

He turned into me, meeting my gaze. "As ready as I'll ever be."

I reached up, placing both hands on his cheeks, and then covered his mouth with mine. A tingle of electric energy crawled over my skin. And as I inhaled, the room turned a pale shade of gray, blocking out everything except for Julius and the strange clove taste of his lips. He was both familiar and strange at the same time. Julius never tasted like cloves. Usually just a hint of vanilla.

Relax, Tru, my other guide, whispered in my mind. *You can do this.*

Only I couldn't. A stabbing pain shot down my throat, followed by a burning sensation that made my eyes water. My throat was closing and I couldn't breathe. Pulling away, I gasped for air, clutching at my throat.

"What happened?" Julius grabbed my arms, panic and worry lining his face.

I glanced up at him through watery eyes and shook my head. "Didn't work."

"She was sabotaged," Jade said, ice radiating from her tone. "Someone cast a spell, and I don't think it was Julius."

"What the… a spell?" Julius asked. Then he sobered, and his body went rigid as he nodded. "Yes, I feel it now. The ghost living inside me used to be a witch."

"You're sure?" Jade asked while I rubbed at my raw throat.

"I'm sure. It's normally used as a defensive spell when being attacked. Like pepper spray."

I wiped at my watering eyes and sucked in a gulp of clean air. "That's what that feels like? Holy hell. I guess he didn't want to leave."

Julius wrapped an arm around me. "I'm sorry, Pyper. That must've been awful."

"It was. But it wasn't your fault, and there doesn't appear to be any lasting damage. I'm just not sure what to do now."

"Well," Jade said, "he must be sticking around for a reason. The only thing we can do is try to figure out who he is and why he might be here, at least until we can get off this ship and either call Lailah or fly back to New Orleans."

We were scheduled to dock in Montego Bay the day after tomorrow. At that time, we could fly back to New Orleans if need be. Until then, we had two days to try to figure out what was going on with Julius and his onboard passenger.

"Where do we start?" I asked.

Kane cleared his throat. "I think the best thing to do is to talk to someone about the history of that room. The ship management and staff. See if we can get anything more than what's in the dossier. Rumors and hearsay often are rooted in truth."

"That sounds like a plan." Jade stood. "How about we split up? Kane and I will talk to the management while you two work on the staff?"

I glanced at Julius. "Are you up for that?"

He nodded. "It's better than sitting here doing nothing."

"Good." Jade glanced at the clock. "It's just past one now. How about we spend the rest of the afternoon investigating and then meet up for dinner and share anything we've learned?"

We agreed, said our good-byes, and left.

"Where to first?" I asked Julius, forcing a chipper tone. If this was the only thing we could do at this point, then I was damn sure going to give it my full attention even if it did feel like we'd be looking for a needle in a haystack. Anyone could've cursed that room at any time. And that included passengers. Not to mention, I'd be surprised if the ship didn't have a fairly high turnover rate with staff. Keeping everything going smoothly sounded daunting.

"It doesn't matter." He sounded exhausted and looked even worse with his pale skin and dark smudges under his eyes. "Anywhere."

"Okay. This way then." I tugged him down the hallway, passing an elderly couple and someone I recognized. Cal. A tall blond woman stood in front of him, her face scrunched up in anger. Beth. His would-be fiancée.

"Don't talk to me right now." She placed her hands on her hips. "I already told you I need time. If you think your half-assed apology is going to make everything better, you've lost your mind. Now leave me alone before I decide to dump your two-timing butt."

He opened his mouth to speak, but she raised her hand in a stop motion and then stalked off down the hallway.

His shoulders slumped as he leaned against the wall, defeated.

"She's not taking the news very well, is she?" I asked gently.

"Nope." He closed his eyes and let out a deep sigh. "She didn't want to hear about the ghost invasion. Said I sounded desperate and juvenile."

Julius glanced at me, his eyebrows raised in question.

"Julius, this is Cal. Cal, Julius." I waved my hand between them for the introduction.

Julius gave the man a short nod. "Rough trip?"

Cal let out a humorless huff of laughter. "You could say that."

"You're not the only one." Julius eyed the man for a moment. Then he pulled out a card and handed it to him. "Our room number is on the back. If you need us to talk to her, we can help with that."

"I don't think anything anyone says is going to convince her. She doesn't believe in ghosts."

The misery on Cal's face nearly broke my heart. "Listen," I said. "We've seen more than the average Joe, a lot more. And I still have trouble believing half the crap that goes down. But when you see it with your own two eyes, it's hard to deny. If she's willing to even entertain the idea that you're telling the truth, bring her by and we'll see if we can't show her something that will turn her into a believer. Or at least get her to believe your story might be possible."

"Show?" he asked, alarm filling his tone.

I chuckled while Julius just stared at me, a slight frown tugging at his lips.

"Don't worry. It wouldn't be anything bad. Just a small spell or illusion is all it would take." I nudged Julius's shoulder, hoping my suggestion wasn't too far over the line. I'd basically offered for Julius to put himself on display while working a spell.

His lack of reaction was better than an outraged one.

"Seriously?" Cal asked, straightening. "You'd do that for me?"

I nodded, not waiting for Julius to respond.

"But why? You don't even know me." He glanced up and down the now empty hallway. Leaning in, he lowered his voice,

"And to be honest, I really don't want to see or meet any ghosts ever again."

"First of all, I'm a closet romantic. So the fact that she's barely speaking to you over something you had no control over breaks my heart. Second, most ghosts aren't so bad. And although it's unlikely, if we could get one to appear, maybe even Bootlegger, you'd have all the proof you needed." I placed a light hand on Julius's arm. "But if that fails, this guy right here has a few tricks up his sleeve that might convince her."

Julius's expression turned into one of resigned indifference.

"I knew you'd get on board," I whispered to him, then turned to Cal. "Remember, if you need us for anything, call or pound on our door. We can help."

Cal stared at the back of the card for a long moment, then stuffed it into his back pocket. "I will."

"Good." I grinned. "We'll talk to you later. Right now Julius and I have somewhere important to be."

Chapter 15

T HE OPEN-AIR BAR set beside the deep blue-lagoon pool buzzed with energy. People smelling of coconut oil, decked out in swimwear, large-brimmed hats, and sunglasses milled around with tropical drinks garnished with pineapples and cherries.

Julius frowned as I led him up to the bar. "I thought we were supposed to be interviewing the staff?"

"Sit," I said, gently nudging him toward a barstool. Then I turned to the middle-aged surfer dude behind the counter. "Two bourbons, neat. Make one a double."

"You got it." He turned, reaching for the shot glasses.

"The good stuff if you have it."

He nodded once, his bleached-blond locks falling into his eyes.

"I'm not sure this is the best idea," Julius said but made no move to leave his stool.

I patted his leg. "I'm pretty sure it's what we both need. One drink isn't going to do any harm. Besides, we can question Moon Doggie here. Kill two birds with one stone."

"Moon Doggie?" The bartender gave me a what-the-hell look as he finished pouring our drinks.

I smiled at him. "You just look so California beach bum. No offense."

He chuckled. "None taken." He pushed the drinks toward us. "Want to start a tab?"

"No," Julius said at the same time I said, "Yes."

Smirking at Julius, I passed my keycard to the bartender. "Charge it to this room."

"Got it." He turned and did something at the register. A second later he was back, handing me my key. "Now, what is it you want to question me about?"

"Two seconds," I said, handing Julius the double shot of bourbon. I clinked my glass to his and raised it in a salute. "Bottoms up."

Julius didn't hesitate. In once swift motion, he tilted the glass and downed the liquid. Instantly the color came back into his cheeks and his eyes brightened.

"That's better," I said and turned back to Surfer Dude. "Can I get a top-shelf margarita, salt, on the rocks? And Julius will have…?"

"A beer. Whatever craft you have on tap. The darker the better."

The bartender went to work, and Julius turned to scan the ship deck. "It must be nice to be on vacation and the only thing to worry about is what to have for dinner."

I let out a startled laugh. "I'm afraid neither of our lives will ever be that calm."

"You're probably right. It sure does make it hard to plan a future though when the crap is always hitting the fan." There was a wistfulness in his tone that sparked a sharp pang of regret in my chest.

He wanted to plan a future? That was news to me. I couldn't help but wonder if that future included me. "Maybe it's better to just take one day at a time right now."

He made a noncommittal sound but nodded his agreement.

Surfer Dude placed our drinks in front of us.

"Thanks." I took a sip and sighed in pleasure. "Damn good margarita."

"I try." He winked and started to move away.

"Hey, you got a second?" I called.

He glanced down the bar at two older ladies in their brightly colored sarongs. They were chatting away, each one appearing to try to outtalk the other. He reclaimed his spot in front of me. "Looks like I do."

I flashed him a bright smile. "Great. Listen, we're doing some work for the cruise line. Just a little paranormal investigating. You know, like that *Ghost Hunters* show on TV?"

"Seriously?" His voice rose with his excitement. "You're joking, right?"

I shook my head. "Not at all. I've done some ghost hunting, mostly in the French Quarter. It appears this ship has a room or two that's been associated with paranormal activity. Have you heard anything about that before? Specifically room 1538?"

"Man! I'd love to be there for the investigation. Back in California I lived in an old converted theater, and I swear a starlet from the forties haunted the place. I used to see her in her stockings and garter—"

I cleared my throat. "That sounds… disruptive."

A slow smile spread over his face. "You could say that."

Oh for Pete's sake. "Sounds interesting. Maybe we can interview you about that later? Right now we're in the middle of an investigation of room 1538. I like to stay focused." I gave him a coy smile.

"Right. Sure. Understandable. When you're done, don't forget to ask me about Claudette. The stories I have…" He chuckled. "They might be R rated. Not safe for the PG crowd, if you know what I mean."

Just what I wanted to hear. Dirty ghost stories from the guy with a Peter Pan syndrome. "I might just have to do that."

There was a slight chill in the air, and a faint tickle brushed my skin just as Ida May appeared next to me. "Sounds delicious. X-rated starlet. I always knew those Hollywood types were freaky."

I gave her a side-eye glance, wondering where she'd been for the past twelve or so hours.

"With Bootlegger of course." She covered her mouth as she giggled.

"You're reading my mind now?" I blurted.

"Huh?" Surfer Dude asked, confused by my apparent one-sided conversation.

"Oh, sorry. Nothing. I was just—Never mind." I glared at Ida May.

"Relax. I know you well enough to know what that look meant. And now you're wondering what ghost sex looks like."

"God, no." I jerked my gaze away from her, hoping if I ignored her, she'd go away. Or at the very least stop talking.

"Are you all right?" Surfer Guy's brows pinched as he stared at me like I'd lost my mind.

"She's fine," Julius interjected. "She sometimes talks to herself when she's working through a problem."

"The ghost hunting?" he asked. "Did you guys find

anything?"

I gave Julius a grateful smile and then turned my attention to Surfer Dude. "Maybe. But now we're trying to fill in the pieces. If you have any information, it would be really helpful."

He pursed his lips. "Other than the usual noises and flickering lights, you mean?"

"Yes. Anything you've seen or heard."

He shrugged. "That room has been cursed for years. The odd thing is that men are the only ones who ever talk about it. They report feeling like they're being watched, shadows in the mirrors, the room feeling stifling even when the air is on full blast. That's all I know really. But you might want to talk to Xavier. He's the maintenance guy assigned to that floor. If anyone knows the history, it's him."

"Thanks." I whipped out my phone and noted Xavier, maintenance. "That was tremendously helpful."

"No problem. Always glad to help a fellow ghost hunter." There was an excited gleam in his eye that at one time I would've encouraged. I'd dated a ghost hunter for a while, and when he'd left town, I'd sort of taken over his role. But now? Mostly I didn't want to get involved unless there was something nefarious going on.

"I didn't realize you were a hunter," Julius said, eyeing him up and down as if a surfer bartender dude couldn't possibly know anything about ghosts. A giggle bubbled up in the back of my throat, but I swallowed it, not wanting to offend our informant.

"Well, just the experience back in California. But it was something else. You should've been there when Claudette decided to strip right down to her—

"Hey, one more thing," I interjected, this time mentally rolling my eyes. I already had one inappropriate ghost. I didn't need to hear about another. But as long as we were here, I figured it wouldn't hurt to ask about a certain ghostly rock star. "We're trying to gather data on Vienna Vox for the memorial celebration. Did you happen to be around during her tragic demise?"

"We are?" Julius asked under his breath.

"Sure," I mumbled back.

Surfer Dude pulled a towel from his back pocket and started wiping the counter as his expression sobered. "I worked on the ship. Yes."

Jackpot!

Julius turned, giving the bartender his full attention. "Did you know her?"

He didn't say anything at first, but then he shook his head. "Know isn't quite the right word. I knew of her. Served her a few times. Heard rumors, but if you're looking for anything more than hearsay, you'd be better off talking to our production manager, Cydney."

"She's in charge of the entertainment?" I guessed.

"Yeah. She's the one who books the acts and keeps the performers happy." He glanced down at the older ladies again as he continued to wipe the same section of the bar.

"The rumors," Julius said, narrowing his eyes. "Can you tell us about those?"

Surfer Dude froze for a second. Then he straightened and rolled his shoulders. "None of that is true. Just a bunch of BS gossip. Nothing worth repeating."

I sucked down the last of my margarita. Shoving my empty

glass toward him, I said, "Oh, I bet you have some good stories. Even if they aren't true, I'd love to hear a good cruise ship tale."

"Do you need a refill?" he asked, relaxing slightly as he gave me a hint of a smile.

"Yes, please. And don't forget to give me the gossip." I rubbed my palms together as if I were full of evil. "I just love a good conspiracy theory."

Julius pulled his wallet out and slid a twenty-dollar tip toward the bartender, further eroding any hesitation Surfer Dude might have had.

After a nod of thanks and pocketing the twenty, he placed his elbows on the bar and leaned down close to us. Lowering his voice to a whisper, he said, "There was a rumor that Muse, her backup singer was carrying a torch for her. That she and Vienna, along with Vienna's boyfriend, Razer, had some sort of agreement."

"What do you mean, 'agreement'"? I asked, eyeing my empty glass. He'd apparently forgotten all about my refill. Heck, at that point, I'd have been happy with just a tequila shot.

"You know, they shared. Vienna was dating them both. Apparently sharing a bed with them both at the same time."

Julius raised his eyebrows, but there was no shock in his expression. More mild curiosity.

I tried not to laugh at Surfer Dude's drama-ridden explanation. Who cared if they were all sleeping with each other? Unless there was a crime of passion. "Okay. Are Muse and Razer still an item?"

He jerked back, surprise in his pale blue eyes. "Razer? No. The night after Vienna was lost, he left the ship when we got into port in Jamaica. He just disappeared. Some people still speculate that he killed her, but no one has seen or heard from him since. Not even Muse."

I bit down on my lower lip as all my alarm bells went off. There had to have been some sort of falling out with the trio. That meant I had to talk to Muse if I wanted to find out what happened between them.

Julius's body tensed slightly. I eyed him noting his knuckles turning white as he gripped the edge of the bar.

"Julius—"

"You know Muse?" Julius asked, his voice suddenly taking on a rasp that wasn't normally there.

"Sure," Surfer Dude said. "She comes back every year on the anniversary of Vox's disappearance. I've even partied with her a few times. Man, that girl can throw back some tequila. And when she gets going—"

"Where can I find her?" Julius's tone was urgent now, almost desperate.

I placed my hand on his arm, but he ignored me as he stared intently at Surfer Dude.

"Uh, her room, maybe? The theater?" He shrugged. "Knowing her, she's probably passed out in some random passenger's bed." Surfer Dude glanced at me. "She's a little promiscuous. Feisty, that one."

Ida May did the eye rolling this time. *"Don't listen to him. She's in her room, hiding from the band."*

I glanced at her and then back at the bartender. He was frowning at Julius.

"Are you okay, man? You look a little upset. Here, let me refill that beer for you." And without waiting for an answer, Surfer Dude finally went to work on our drinks.

"Want to tell me what that was about?" I asked Julius.

"Huh?" He tore his gaze away from the beer Surfer Dude was pouring to glance at me.

I sucked in a small startled breath as I stared into brilliant blue eyes.

Eyes that didn't belong to Julius.

Chapter 16

BEFORE I COULD say anything, Surfer Dude was back with our drinks. "So what's the plan? Are you two doing any more investigating today?"

"Maybe." I hedged, trying to be as vague as possible. Our ploy to use ghost hunting as a cover was backfiring.

"Great!" Surfer Dude glanced at the clock. "I get off at two. I'd love to come observe if you don't mind. I know all about EMF detectors and gathering data. I could set stuff up, hold the video camera, anything. Just let me know what I can do."

Crap on a cracker. The last thing we needed was an amateur hunter getting in the way. We didn't have time for that. "I think we're just conducting interviews today. Maybe next time."

I jumped to my feet and grabbed the edge of the bar when dizziness kicked in. Whoa. Those drinks had been stronger than I'd realized. Of course, we also hadn't eaten lunch.

"Well, if you change your mind, just come by the bar. Whoever is here can get in touch with me."

"Yeah, sure." I tugged on Julius's arm.

He slid off the stool, beer in hand, his eyes still blazing blue. He let me lead him away, but he didn't speak and kept sweeping his gaze back and forth over the deck as if searching for something.

Spotting a deserted corner in the shade, I made a beeline for the table. "Sit," I ordered Julius as I sat across from him.

He didn't respond.

I stifled a sigh. "Julius?"

Still no response.

A twinge of panic pinched my gut. Time for a new tactic. "Who are you looking for?"

"My girlfriend," he said, squinting into the sun. "Have you seen her?"

Yes. She's right here, I wanted to scream, but it was clear to me whoever was speaking through Julius definitely wasn't Julius. "Maybe. Who's your girlfriend again?"

"She's missing," he said.

"Okay. When did she go missing?"

A muscle in his jaw started to pulse. "Last night."

"At the chocolate competition?"

He finally turned to stare at me, anger flickering through his steely gaze. "What are you talking about? She was in the elevator. You were there."

Oh holy hell! The image of the woman singing in the moonlight flashed in my mind followed by her reaching out to Julius. Only she hadn't been seeing him, she'd been seeing whoever was possessing him. My heart started to pound, and I sucked in a sharp breath, regaining my composure. "You're looking for Vienna Vox."

He nodded once and scanned the deck again.

I replayed what he'd said. He was looking for his girlfriend. How could that be? The bartender said Razer had gotten off the ship right after Vienna had disappeared, that he'd never spoken to Muse again. But what if he hadn't left? What if he'd been trapped in room 1538 for the past ten years?

"Razer?" I asked.

"What?" he barked out, then downed half the beer before placing the mug back on the table.

Son of a mother. That explained why Julius had called Vienna *Vivi* the night before and why he couldn't remember leaving the chocolate party. Julius had been taken over by Vienna Vox's boyfriend. Presumably the prime suspect in her murder. I stood abruptly, knocking the beer over. Dark liquid spilled over the table and dripped onto the deck.

He stared up at me, puzzled. "Going somewhere?"

Was I? I took a tiny step back and shook my head. I couldn't leave. Couldn't let Julius out of my sight. Swallowing my panic, I sat back down. "Sorry about the beer."

He glanced at the still-dripping liquid. "I can get another one."

I supposed that was true, but he didn't move. And neither did I. What was the best way to proceed? Just ask him if he knew what was going on? Pretend this was completely normal? Run screaming across the ship to Jade?

"You're taking this awfully well," he said.

A high-pitched giggle sounded from behind me. I turned and glared at Ida May. She'd finally left the bar and whatever tourist she'd been drooling over this time. Ignoring her, I turned back around. "You realize you've invaded Julius's body then?"

He nodded once. "That couldn't be helped."

I let out an irritated huff. "I think maybe we could've found a better solution."

"Yeah, like turning him over to me," Ida May said, fanning herself. "Hot damn. He's hot!"

"Thank you," Razer said, nodding in Ida May's direction.

She let out a gasp, then squealed. "You can hear me?"

"Sure. I am a ghost after all." He ran his gaze down the length of her body, nodding in approval. "Nice legs."

"Thank you." She brushed her thick curly hair back and all but preened. "Nice tats. Dragons are so sexy."

"Tats?" I peered at him, seeing nothing, not even a freckle on Julius's tanned arms. And hadn't she called him hot? How did she know? Razer might have invaded Julius's body, but he still looked like Julius.

Ida May floated next to him, running her finger along his forearm. "Right here. This is the head and then the fire."

I concentrated on his arm, imagining brightly colored scales and a piercing dragon eye. After a moment, the dragon began to take shape. It was red and orange with a yellow eye. Fire blazed around his wrist. The same design I'd seen earlier when Jade had used magic to reveal the hidden tattoo.

Raising my gaze, I blinked. Julius wasn't standing there at all. In his place was a tall, lanky guy with shaggy, shoulder-length hair. He had a row of piercings on his right ear and only one on the left.

He held out his hand. "I'm Razer. And you are?"

Stunned, I automatically clasped his hand, shaking it. "Pyper Rayne. I'm a medium."

I had no idea why I'd felt it necessary to divulge that information, but there it was.

He dropped my hand and shoved his into his pockets, his expression all business. "Have you seen Vienna?"

I nodded slowly. "A couple of times last night."

"She's dead, isn't she?" The question was matter-of-fact, devoid of emotion.

"Of course she is," Ida May answered for me.

He jerked his head to glare at her. And I swear if looks could kill, Ida May would've died a second death right there near the blue lagoon pool.

She held her hands up and floated away from him. "Sorry. Didn't realize you'd be so touchy about it. It's been ten years."

"Ten years!" His eyes went wide in shock as the blood drained from his face. Then he sank back down into the chair, his shoulders hunched and his expression stricken.

"Ida May, go away," I said, completely annoyed.

"But—"

"No. You've done quite enough. Now isn't the time." I waved a hand as if to shoo her away. "Razer, what is the last thing you remember before last night? Before you saw Vienna in the elevator?"

His brow furrowed in concentration. "I don't know."

"Do you remember joining with Julius?" What I really wanted to know was if it had been a conscious effort and if he was here to stay. Or was he just as much a victim of circumstance as Julius was?

Silence stretched between us.

Ida May had moved to lie in a lounge chair, her head tilted up to the sun as if she could feel the warm rays. Maybe she could. A small pang of jealousy surprised me. The idea of lounging near the pool without a care in the world sounded like heaven. But only if I had Julius with me. And right now, even though he was literally sitting across from me, he was unreachable. I had to figure out how to bring him back to the surface, to push Razer back until we found a way to separate the pair of them.

"How did you end up trapped in that room?" I asked.

"I don't know," he said, his voice so faint I almost didn't hear him.

"Razer?" I peered at him. His lanky frame morphed to Julius's more built one and then back again.

When he spoke this time, his tone was stronger, full of confidence as his brilliant blue eyes blazed with passion. "I tried to save her. I was too late."

Nervous energy had me tapping my foot. "You saw what happened to her?"

He shook his head, sadness radiating from him. "I warned her she was in danger. Knew I should've stayed with her, but we had a fight. By the time I shook my anger off, she was already gone. It's my fault she died."

"But you weren't there—"

"Exactly." He ran a hand across the back of his neck. "I don't remember anything after I went after her killer. At least not until I stepped into this body."

My eyes widened and my pulse sped up. "You know who did it."

But again he shook his head. "I never saw his face. But I knew he was the one. He had the necklace her mother gave her. The one she never took off."

I sat back in my chair, processing what he'd said. Then my heart nearly broke. What an awful thing to endure.

Those tortured eyes met mine, and what I saw there nearly tore me in two. Pain so raw it brought tears to my eyes. Then he spoke. "I was going to ask her to marry me that night." His voice cracked when he continued. "But we got into a stupid fight. I never did ask. She stormed off, and it was the last time I saw her."

I reached for him, unable to keep my distance. And the minute my hand covered his, the air shimmered between us. Razer's image blurred, and just like that Julius was back.

He stood abruptly and came around the table to stand in front of me. "Pyper?"

I blinked the tears from my eyes, already reaching for his hand. "Julius?"

Our fingers entwined, his warm hand solid in my chilled one. He pulled me to him, our joined hands smashed between us as we clutched at each other.

His rapidly beating heart thundered beneath my ear, mine thumping just as fast as his.

"I can't believe that just happened," I said, my voice muffled from his shirt.

He let out a humorless chuckle. "Sadly, I can. But at least now I know why I was dreaming of Vienna. They weren't my dreams. They were his."

I pulled away slightly to glance up at him. With his history, from being a ghost for a century and being in and out of limbo much of that time, I supposed he could believe just about anything.

"What are we going to do?" I asked. "You can't live like this, with him taking over whenever he feels like it."

"You're right." He stroked my hair absently. "He's not leaving until he has answers, and he's relying on me to find them."

A cold chill ran through my veins. "He wants you to solve Vienna's murder?"

"Yes." His tone was matter-of-fact, but Julius's body tensed and he took a step back, putting distance between us.

There was more. I felt it deep in my bones. "And?"

His jaw tightened. "He's determined to get revenge."

Chapter 17

GARLIC WAFTED FROM the plate of mashed potatoes and perfectly prepared filet. Julius, who was for the time being in full possession of himself, was to my right, Jade to my left, and Kane across from me. After our lunch of cocktails and gossip, we'd desperately needed food.

I was halfway through my steak before I glanced up, noticing Kane staring at me with an awed expression on his face. "What?"

He glanced down at his plate. The fish he'd ordered hadn't yet been disturbed. "I'm just impressed at your Hoover abilities. And your metabolism. For a woman as tiny as you, that's quite the show you're putting on."

"Kane!" Jade swatted his arm. "Be nice."

I waved a hand, indicating I didn't care what he said. "You're just jealous of my girlish figure."

Julius let out a chuckle and quickly covered his mouth with a napkin.

"If you say so," Kane said, smiling.

"I'm going to need a side of truffle fries," I said to no one in particular. "Someone wave a server down, will you?" Conducting a ten-year-old murder investigation through ghosts was hard work.

"We found something interesting," Jade said, suddenly all business.

I put my fork down and gave her my full attention. During the appetizers, we'd already filled them in on the fact that Razer was the one sharing Julius's body and that we'd "met" him today. And we'd made a plan to hunt down Xavier and Cydney the next morning. "What?"

"The paranormal activity in room 1538 started not long after Vienna's death. Six months maybe." Jade slathered a generous portion of butter on a piece of herbed bread.

I sat back in my chair. "So? It's a weird coincidence, but six months is a long time for activity to start if it has anything to do with her murder, isn't it?"

Jade shrugged, but Julius and Kane were both shaking their heads.

I glanced at Julius. "It's not?"

"No," Kane answered for him. "Spells, especially dark ones, take time to settle in and start to break down."

"Right," Julius added. "It's quite possible the spell started to deteriorate around the six-month mark, leading to complaints that slowly escalated over the years." Julius was quiet for a moment, appearing to concentrate on something across the room. Then he blinked. "Razer says at some point the magic binding him started to unravel, and that's when he first started trying to escape."

My eyes widened in surprise. "You're talking to him?"

Julius nodded, his expression somber. "Yeah. We're still adjusting, but he can speak in my mind while I'm the dominant player. I suppose I can do the same if he takes over." A small shudder ran through him as he closed his eyes. "Not that I'll let him gain control again. If I hadn't been half-drunk, it wouldn't have happened in the first place."

I opened my mouth to protest but closed it, realizing he was probably right.

Jade leaned forward, her eyes sparkling with interest. "Does he know how he got there?"

Julius shook his head. "No. All he remembers is going after Vienna's killer. The person had the necklace she always wore. The one her mother had given her right after her first paying gig. She never took it off. The rest of the details are vague both before and after."

Jade pressed her lips together in a thin line. "I'm really interested in why he was trapped in that room. It's unusual."

"Razer's a witch, right?" I speculated. "As a ghost he can wreak plenty of havoc, I'm assuming. I suppose he was trapped as a way to keep him under control."

"Maybe," she said quietly.

"While I agree it would be interesting to know those details, there's something else," Kane said. "Room 1538 was assigned to Muse during that trip. Not Vienna and Razer. They were on an entirely different floor."

I sucked in a sharp gasp of air. "She knows something. I'm certain of it."

"And she's refused to stay not just in that room, but on that floor every year when she comes back for the anniversary," Kane added.

We were all silent as we let that sink in. The waiter came back around, filling our water and wineglasses. The new information had me distracted, and I forgot to order my truffle fries.

As he walked away, I raised my hand to call him back but gave up when Julius said, "Razer needs to talk to her."

"Now?" I stared at my half-eaten steak, disappointment settling in.

"After we finish eating," Kane said and shoved a forkful of crab-stuffed flounder into his mouth.

"Thank goodness." I dug into my food and didn't come up for air until my plate was clean and I'd finished off the flourless chocolate cake that had magically appeared on the table.

"Wow," Jade said. There was a teasing smile on her face as she eyed my empty plates. "That was impressive, even for you."

I grinned. "Good food. Good company. And I was starving."

"Did you get enough?" Kane asked seriously.

"I think so. At least for now." I chuckled to myself. Ladylike wasn't exactly high on my priority list, though I did know how to turn on the charm when it was necessary. Dinner with the Rouquettes and Julius wasn't one of those times. They got the real me, no filters, and I loved them for loving me anyway. Standing, I held my hand out to Julius.

He had dark smudges under his eyes, and his face was paler than usual. Exhaustion must've been setting in. Living with someone else in your skin really took a toll. The fact that he'd waited for me to finish my dinner without complaint made my heart swell with admiration. He had to be anxious for answers.

"Ready?" I asked him.

He nodded once as he stood. He slipped his hand into mine, and we followed Jade and Kane out of the restaurant.

I slowed my pace, putting distance between them and us.

When I was reasonably certain they were out of earshot, I wrapped my hands around Julius's arm and gazed up at him. "Are you sure you're doing all right?"

There was a bit of weariness in his eyes. "I'll be fine. Just need some rest."

I placed my head against his shoulder, wishing I could do something more to help him. "Now that we know Razer is a ghost and not a lost soul, we could ask Jade if she can try a couple of spells to separate you."

He let out a breath. "We could, but I don't think I want to."

I stopped, surprise rooting me to the floor. "Why not? I know how hard that is. I've been there."

"Because I know what it's like to be a ghost. To fade in and out of consciousness. To be one step out of reality. To not have a real sense of time. And Razer needs to see this through. I'm pretty sure given enough time, he'll remember important details or be the key to solving this murder. And without me, without my stability, he could be lost again. We might never learn the truth, and neither of them will be at peace."

Tears burned the back of my eyes at the emotion in his gruff tone. His time as a ghost had been rougher on him than I'd imagined. And even though he was here now, he'd never forget and wouldn't forgive himself if he didn't help Razer. "You're a good man, Julius."

"Not really." A small smile tugged at his lips. "I just have a debt or two to pay forward."

"No, you don't." I knew he'd always feel responsible for the death of the women he'd failed to save the night of his first death. But we both knew it wasn't his fault. She'd come back as a ghost and had confirmed that just a few weeks ago. That didn't change the fact he'd gotten a second lease on life and wasn't going to take that for granted. My heart swelled with pride and something very close to love.

He started to say something, but I cut him off. "I firmly believe you don't owe anyone anything for what happened all those years ago, but I understand being grateful and doing what you can to help Razer and Vienna. And I admire you for it."

"Not nearly as much as I admire you and your strength," he whispered and bent to kiss the top of my head. "The lengths you go to in order to help people is remarkable. Especially since you don't have magic. Most people wouldn't."

I didn't think that was true at all. In fact, I preferred to believe that most people were kind and willing to do a lot more than they were given credit for. Unfortunately, we were always dealing with the bad guys, and that tended to cloud our judgement. "I think when the crap hits the fan, most people would surprise you."

"They surprise me all right," he grumbled.

I chuckled. "I meant in a good way. Lightly tapping his forearm, I jerked my head toward the Rouquettes, who were now waiting for us near the elevators. "Come on. Let's catch up. We have a rock star to talk to."

✧   ✧   ✧

I GLANCED AT the room number. 1901. Was it just the night before when we'd found Muse falling-down drunk? Hopefully she hadn't spent the day throwing back shots at the bar like we had. We really needed a coherent Muse if we wanted to get anywhere.

"You're sure this is it?" Julius asked.

Jade nodded. "Positive. We saw her come out of this room last night and the manager of Guest Services confirmed it. I have the room numbers for the entire band and anyone on board who might have known Vienna. But Muse's room is by far the best starting point."

"All right then." Julius stood with his shoulders straight as if he was braced for something and then rapped on the door three times.

I heard a rumbling on the other side of the gray door but then silence.

He knocked again, this time harder, as he called, "Muse?"

The door swung open. Muse clutched the door, her ankles wobbling on her too-high boots. Her eyes were glassy and she had a sloppy grin on her face. "Hey! Looks like the party found me."

"Um, not exactly," Jade said.

"Oh sure you did." She held the door wide open, teetering dangerously to the left. She wore a short leather skirt and a beaded silver top. Just the type of outfit one would expect from a rocker. "Come in. I've got plenty to go around. Just opened a fresh bottle. Drinking's not destructive if it's social, right?"

Jade and I shared a worried glance as we stepped into her oversized suite. She was already plowed.

"Drinks for everyone!" Muse swept her arm out in a grand display, sending three bottles crashing to the floor. She stood there for a moment, staring at the mess, a blank expression on her face.

I let out a sigh, and together Jade and I bent to start cleaning up the broken glass.

Muse started to giggle. "Oops. That wasn't supposed to happen."

"Julius? Can you grab the trash bucket from the bathroom?" I asked.

But he didn't answer me. His eyes had turned brilliant blue again and he was moving straight toward Muse with his arms out.

She stumbled back a step, clearly taken by surprise.

But Julius—or rather Razer—didn't stop. He swept her up in his arms, lifting her off her feet as he gave her one hell of a bear hug.

She let out a startled shriek. "Hey! Put me down."

Razer just laughed and twirled her around. "Damn, are you a sight for very sore eyes."

"Can I get some help here?" There was panic in her tone now. And before I could move, she started kicking and screaming. "Let me down, you creep. I don't know who you think you are, but this is unacceptable."

He quickly put her down and held his hands up as he backed away. "It's me, Musey. Razer."

Her brow furrowed, and a flash of anger lit her dark eyes. "This isn't funny." She turned to me. "You people are terrible. Get out!"

"Muse—" Jade started as she moved toward her.

"No. I want you to leave now." She bent over and stumbled, falling to one knee, but still managed to grab a stray stiletto and held it up, brandishing the heel in our direction. "You're sick and twisted. Razer—" Her words got caught on a sob and she shook her head, a tear rolling down her cheek.

"Listen." Razer bent down so he could stare her in the eye.

"I know this seems crazy. But look at me. Really look at me."

There must've been something in his voice or gentle tone that calmed her, because she did as he asked, staring into those brilliant blue eyes. She let out a small gasp and slowly lowered her shoe.

He gave her a tiny, wry smile, and pushed up his sleeve, revealing the distinctive dragon tattoo. "It's me, Bella Muse. I'm here."

Her mouth worked as her eyes darted between Jade and me. "How..." She reached up and gently laid her fingertips on his stubbled cheek. "What happened to you? Where have you been?"

"I've been here all along, my friend. Just detained." He stood and held a hand out to her. "Come. There's much to talk about."

Uncertainty clouded her expression, and she gave a tiny shake of her head as the fierceness returned to her steely gaze. "I'm not going anywhere with anyone. You might have Razer's eyes and his tattoos, but I know better than to believe anything without proof." Her hand tightened around her stiletto again as she pushed herself to her feet, surprisingly steady after her recent drunken display.

Razer raised both eyebrows, and then without a word he retreated to the couch and sat down at the end. "Proof? How about your birthday is June twenty-first? We were officially introduced to each other at a studio session Vienna put together when she wanted to record 'Naked Souls.' But we first met at a frat party at LSU two years before. You were dressed up as a sexy Glinda the Good Witch. Vienna was dressed as the Red Queen. And I'd been trying to get a date with you for over an hour before you blew me off for Gerald Veauxzoo. Ten minutes later, Vienna took pity on me and bought me a beer. The next day you took off for New York City, and by the time you got back, Vivi and I were already living together. You told me once I was the nerdy guy that got away right before you left the bar with a man in a kilt. You told us we didn't want to know what he was wearing underneath because adult diapers—"

She let out a squeal of delight and launched herself at him, wrapping both arms and legs around him, holding on so tight I thought she'd strain something.

He laughed, holding on just as tightly.

I cleared my throat. "Um, guys? I don't want to ruin the reunion, but we do have some things to discuss." It wasn't that I was jealous, exactly. I knew Razer and Muse were overwhelmed and excited to see each other. But it was still weird to see Julius's body wrapped around another woman.

Razer stood, and Muse slowly slid down his body. She kept her hand on his cheek as she stared up at him. "Where exactly have you been? I thought…" Her lower lip turned white as she bit down. "Why do you look like some hipster douche?"

Jade let out a startled giggle. I sucked in a sharp breath, not appreciating at all her assessment of Julius's old-school 1920s look. There was nothing wrong with cuffed pants, a white button-down shirt, and leather shoes. In fact, I thought his checkered suspenders were just the right amount of quirky fun.

Razer's expression darkened. "It's a long story, but the short version is I battled Vivi's murderer and lost. My business wasn't at all finished, and I immediately came back as a ghost. But the other witch spelled me into the walls of your room, 1538."

Muse's entire body had gone stock-still as she stared at him, but when he'd said 1538, a noticeable tremor shuddered through her.

He reached out, rubbing her shoulder as if soothing her. "I've been there ever since, until last night when Julius here broke the spell. Something strange happened, and the next thing I knew, we were sharing his body." He glanced down, something between a grimace and a wry smile tugging at his lip. "Old-school suspenders and all."

Her lips quirked up into a small half smile. And so did his.

After a moment she reached for him but then froze as her face went completely white and she grabbed the back of the chair to her left. She clutched so hard her knuckles went white.

"Muse?" he asked, wariness clear in his tone.

A pained expression washed over her face as she squeezed her eyes shut. When she opened them, she choked out, "You have to leave. Get away from me. It's not safe."

"What?" His brow furrowed as he reached for her again.

But she took several steps back, violently shaking her head. "He'll know. And he'll destroy you all. All of you."

"Who?" I asked, my breath getting caught in the back of my throat. Holy hell. Was the killer on the ship? Had he been here all along? I leaned in, impatient for the answer.

But all she did was shake her head. "I can't tell you."

"Of course you can. Who is he? I'll protect you," Razer said, glancing around the room as if the threat was only a few feet away.

"No. I mean I physically can't. He spelled me." Tears shone in her defeated eyes. "And if you stay on the ship, I'll have no choice but to tell him you're here."

Jade peered at her and let out a small grunt of frustration.

"He's definitely here then. And I'm guessing a simple silencing spell isn't the only nasty thing he's hit you with."

Muse nodded, then grabbed her head and screamed bloody murder. When she finally stopped, her face had gone from white to green and she shook her head violently. "No. Just go. Get off at the next port of call. There's nothing for any of you to do."

"I know that's not true," Jade said gently. "I can feel it."

She covered her head with her hands and slid to the floor, the hopelessness practically radiating from her. "Just go. Just go. Just go," she said over and over again, rocking back and forth like a child.

Razer sat on the floor next to her, wrapping his arm around her shoulders. "You're not alone anymore, Mia. I'm here. No more carrying the weight of this on your shoulders. I won't let you."

She stopped suddenly, and with her expression clear, she stared him in the eye and said, "Don't call me Mia. That girl died the night I lost my best friend and the man I called brother."

So much for Surfer Dude's theory that the three of them were a couple. The idea of it made my stomach roll as I watched them and the raw, tragic pain they still suffered. Vienna's memory deserved more than gossip-filled rumors.

Muse peered up at Razer, tears standing in her eyes. And when she finally spoke again, her voice cracked. "The night I stood by and let Vienna die."

Chapter 18

RAZER STIFFENED AT her words. Then he shook his head. "You didn't do this. It's not—"

"Not what? My fault?" She exploded. "Of course it was my fault." She jumped to her feet, surprisingly agile considering her earlier inebriated state. "I knew he was obsessed with her. He warned me he wasn't going to give up, that she would be his one way or another, that he'd make her see reason. I saw the crazy in his expression. I might not have known he would kill her, but I sure as hell knew deep down inside that he was dangerous. And still I stood by and did nothing. Said nothing. I let my own ego and wounded pride get in the way. And then I lost everything that ever mattered to me. So yeah, it is my fault. And I've been paying for it ever since."

The entire room was dead silent after her outburst. The five of us barely moved—heck, we barely breathed. I wanted to reach out to the broken and battered woman, but her expression was so fierce it was clear comfort wasn't what she needed.

"We can help you," I said, my voice strong and confident. "We can help you defeat the bastard who did this."

Her eyes narrowed. "No one can help me."

"I can," Jade said, her own fierceness streaming off her in

waves.

"So can I," Julius said.

I turned to him, recognizing his soft, determined tone. His eyes had turned back to green, and he had the quiet confidence I'd grown to admire so much. A small knot in my gut eased, one I hadn't even realized was there. Having Razer be in charge was disconcerting on many levels, but there was no denying that every time he took over, that unease wound its way in until Julius returned.

"You have no idea what you're talking about," Muse said, but the conviction in her tone had vanished, leaving only weariness.

"Actually, I have some experience with breaking curses," Jade said softly. "I can't promise I can break yours. Not without knowing the details anyway. But if you're willing to work with me, explain how you're affected, I can certainly give it one heck of a try. And with Julius here to help, there's a good chance we can break it for good."

A faint trace of hope flickered in her eyes but vanished just as quickly. "How do I know I can trust you?"

Jade and I shared a glance.

I shrugged. There wasn't any good way to answer that question. "You don't. But do you have anything to lose? Would you rather stay spelled by this bastard or take a chance at getting your life back?"

"It's only for one week a year," she said almost to herself, then shuddered.

"And you can't tell us who it is?" Jade pushed. "Not even a hint?"

She wrapped her arms around herself and shook her head.

"No. It hurts too much."

"Then why do you come back here?" I asked, not caring if I was being rude. Politeness had no place here. Black magic and evil, murdering witches trumped social niceties.

"I have no choice." The darkness in her tone sent a shiver up my spine. "Every year. Same time, same place, same—" Her voice cut out as her mouth worked. Angry tears welled in her eyes as she clenched her fists and grit her teeth. Finally she forced out, "That's all I can say."

Jade stood and held her hand out to the woman. "That's it. We're doing this. Right here, right now. I will not stand by and watch this happen. One way or another, we're breaking this curse."

Julius shifted to stand shoulder to shoulder with Jade. He, too, held his hand out. "Let us do what we can to help you."

The tension in her shoulders eased and she took a step forward, seemingly willing for the first time, but there was still that wariness that clung to her. "Fine. But I don't understand why you want to do anything for me."

"Because we all have our own crap, our own demons we've had to deal with." I glanced briefly at Kane and then Jade, the two people who'd saved my life more than once, and felt a tightening in my chest. "None of us would be here without each other. Consider it a paying-it-forward type thing."

Kane draped his arm over my shoulders the same way he had a million times before and pulled me to him in a brotherly hug. He didn't say anything, but I felt his love all the way down into my soul. I'd do anything for them. Anything at all. And I knew without a doubt they'd lay their lives down for me. That wasn't something I ever wanted to take for granted. Looking at the girl in front of me, it was clear she'd been on her own for the past decade. That was going to change right this instant.

I turned to Jade. "Okay, boss lady. What do you need from us?"

She stepped back and waved an arm. "Form a circle. I'll take north, Julius south, and you and Kane fill in east and west. Muse?" She turned to the rocker. "You stand in the middle."

"You think a circle is likely to work on the ship?" Julius asked even as he took his position opposite her.

"We're about to find out." She glanced around the room, appearing to look for something, but then shook her head. "I don't suppose you have any sage or salt do you?"

Muse raised one curious eyebrow. "Sage? You're kidding right? You want to smudge away my curse?"

Jade let out a small snort of amusement. "No, obviously that won't work, but it does cleanse the air, make it a little easier to focus."

"Oh, for the love of…" Muse stalked over to the gleaming wood dresser, yanked a drawer open, and waved a hand. "Take your pick. But I've got to tell you, I've already tried burning every herb conceivable, and nothing has worked. Well, there was that one…" She flashed a hint of a wry smile. "But all it did was dull my senses and make me hungry. At least I had something else to focus on for a while."

"I bet," I said, smiling, encouraged to see her spunk coming back. "Herbs or no, I'm confident these two have something up their sleeves that will work."

"I hope so." All her seriousness returned. "Because if he gets wind of this, there's going to be hell to pay."

Jade grabbed a container of salt, sage, and jasmine from

Muse's stash. "Let's see him try." She shot a glance at Kane.

He nodded, a silent message passing between them. Without speaking, he took the salt from her and started pouring it out in a wide circle.

I glanced at Julius, wondering if we'd ever get to the point of practically reading each other's minds. And did I even want that? He reached out and brushed a light hand over my arm, a small gesture that sent a shot of warmth to my belly. Yes, as a matter of fact, I did want that. Even if we had to fight demons and evil to get there.

"What can I do?" I asked Jade.

"Here. Smash these jasmine leaves." She handed me the herbs and nodded to a mortar and pestle sitting in the middle of Muse's dresser.

I grabbed it, noted the burned ashes in the bottom. One whiff told me exactly what Muse had been using it for. Nothing like a little Mary Jane incense to liven up the party. After cleaning the mortar out as best I could and replacing the contents with ground jasmine, I handed it to Muse. "Hold on to this."

Jade was busy smudging the air with sage smoke, asking all unwelcome visitors to please exit the room. Kane had finished the salt circle and pulled the drapes. Julius's job had been to create light orbs that were floating above the circle. The room felt lighter, cleaner, more inviting than it had when Muse had let us in. Clearly the sage had worked.

"Ready?" Jade asked, taking her place on the northern point.

Julius, Kane, and I got into position while Muse stood in the middle of the circle, holding the jasmine.

"Ready," we echoed in unison.

"Perfect." Jade met Julius's gaze. "I'm going to need you to take the lead after I get this going. I think Razer's connection to Muse will help."

"Sure," Julius said. "Just say the word."

Jade closed her eyes and took in a long, slow breath. The temperature in the room seemed to rise a few degrees, and the scent of jasmine intensified. The sweet floral fragrance tickled my nose and put me at ease at the same time.

"From north to south to east to west, I—Jade Calhoun of the New Orleans coven—ask the sea to hear my request. Release Muse from the ties that bind. Let this be a new beginning. From north to south to east to west, grant her freedom from her decade-long test."

Magic crackled from Jade's outstretched fingertips and around our small circle. I closed my own eyes, welcoming the electric current that passed through me to Julius. I felt rather than saw him straighten when her magic engulfed him. And I knew when I opened my eyes he'd be illuminated in her brilliant white light.

"That's it," Jade called over the crackling of magic now filling the room.

My eyes flew open, and my gaze landed on Muse. She was standing with one hand on her hip, holding the jasmine bowl with the other, her expression still skeptical. I almost laughed out loud. She had zero faith.

But then Jade called, "Now!"

Julius opened his mouth as if he were going to speak, but instead, pure white smoke spilled from him, curling and stretching as it snaked its way around the circle, engulfing each of us before the smoke stilled and hung in place. Then all at once it shot toward Muse.

The smoke slammed into her, and she let out a startled cry as she froze in place.

"From north to south to east to west," Jade started chanting, her electric magic pouring into me. Static filled my senses, and I no longer heard her or Julius. My attention was glued to Muse. Her eyes were huge saucers, bloodshot, and filled with terror.

"Stop!" I tried to call out, but my voice was silenced when a loud boom shattered through the room.

The room, Julius, Jade, and Kane faded away, leaving only Muse and me. And right there, standing between us, was the outline of a tall blond man. The smoke still clinging to Muse suddenly shot from her to the man, leaving him in solid form. He had pale blue eyes and three ragged scars that ran from his temple down to his jawline.

An evil smile played at the corners of his mouth as he looked me over. "Looks like Muse brought me a present."

I snarled at her abuser. "Your days of torturing women are over."

He eyed me with interest. "You think so?"

"Jade is going to send you straight to hell."

He tapped a finger to his chin. "That could be interesting. But somehow I don't think today is the day."

Muse stood behind him, her eyes closed and her fists clenched into tight balls, the jasmine bowl discarded on the floor. She was silently chanting something to herself, but I couldn't make out her words.

"You have no idea who you're dealing with," I finally shot back.

The apparition reached back for Muse, but just as he

seemed to touch her, she stepped back and shouted, "No!"

Another man appeared, tall, angry blue eyes, a familiar dragon tattoo winding around his arm.

Razer.

His arms went around Muse, protecting her, as another flash of brilliant white light lit up the circle.

Razer's face contorted with hatred and rage as he stared at Muse's abuser. "Xavier, I should've known it was you. You traitorous, backstabbing, bastard."

"You never were a quick one, were you," Xavier shot back, his tone taking on an air of superiority. "I saw you, you know. Witnessed your pathetic little reunion last night. Too bad I fixed it so the elevator closed on you. Now you'll never see her again."

I let out a startled gasp. He was the maintenance worker who'd been in the corridor with us, who Vienna had pointed at just before he disappeared into the room marked Employees Only. She hadn't been pointing at Julius at all. Everything was starting to make sense now.

"Your time here is over," Razer shot back. "You'll never touch Muse again. Try it and your suffering will be endless."

Xavier shook his head in pity. "I never did figure out what Vienna saw in you."

Razer let out an earsplitting roar, raised one hand and pointed at the man in front of me. "An eye for an eye, your life is forfeit. From today until evermore, you shall be haunted by your sin. Between life and death, your soul is fated for unrest."

Magic crackled around us, and the man in front of me started to fade. His expression contorted into rage as he snarled at Razer and Muse. "You have no idea what you just did."

Razer didn't flinch. "I know exactly what I've done. You'll live forever, in limbo, suffering day in and day out until I release you from your prison."

I felt my lips turn up into a slow, satisfied smile. Good for Razer. Once Kane got around to sending Xavier off to hell, the result would likely be the same, but it had to feel good to be the one to spell the bastard into unrest.

Peering through the fog, I strained to see or even hear my friends. But the static was still drowning out their voices. I caught a whisper of conversation from Muse and Razer, but no one else.

My vision had narrowed to the few feet in front of me, the brilliant magic making it impossible for me to identify anything else. Everything seemed to come to a complete stop as if time had stood still. A prickle of unease trickled up my arms until the hair on the back of my neck stood up.

I gave an involuntary shiver as I watched Xavier morph once again from his shady figure into a solid man. He stood in front of me, his eyes crazed and his lips twisted into a maniacal grin. "Ready, love?"

I had to force myself to not take a step back. Jade formed circles for a reason when she did spell work. To break it now could mean disaster. "Are you ready?" I asked, certain Kane would step up any minute and banish this guy to hell where he belonged.

"More than you possibly could know." He reached out, grabbing my wrist. The burning sensation on my skin startled me, and this time I did take a step back. His eyes glowed with triumph, and just like that my world spun and I was bathed in darkness.

Moments later, my feet slammed into hard concrete. I crumpled, landing on a cold floor, fluorescent lights nearly blinding me.

Xavier grabbed my wrists, and before I could yank them away, I felt rough metal clamp around them, followed by the sinister click of metal locking in place.

I jerked, trying to get away, and was yanked back.

Panic welled up from deep inside me as I glanced up, my gaze locking on my wrists. Rusted manacles held them, tethering me to the metal wall.

Xavier loomed over me, a pleased smile spread across his scarred face. "Welcome to your new home, Ms. Rayne."

Chapter 19

BE CALM, I told myself as I studied the small room. The lightly tinged gray walls had metal brackets holding them together. The cement floor was painted beige, and the shop lighting flickered in and out as if there might be a short in the wiring. No windows, yet I could tell by the slight rocking that we were still on the ship.

Thank the gods.

Julius and the others would find me. There were only so many places one could be on this bucket of bolts.

"I imagine this didn't turn out the way you planned." Xavier was sprawled on a black leather love seat on the other side of the room. An iPod dock sat on a round metal table at the end of the love seat.

I frowned. What the hell kind of weird crap was this creeper into? "Why me?"

"Because those witches broke the spell on Muse. I imagine they weren't expecting her to go into a magically induced coma."

Last I'd seen her, she was awake and being held by Razer. I rolled my shoulders, trying to ease some of the tension. Holding my arms over my head was going to get old really fast. "She looked fine to me," I said defiantly. "And now that the spell is broken, it's only a matter of time before the hunt is on. If you think you're going to get away with holding me here—"

"Oh, Ms. Rayne. We are going to have some fun. It's been years since Muse has shown such spark."

"Years?" I twisted my wrists, testing the manacles, and ground my teeth against the sharp scraping of my skin.

"Ten. But that's not important. Right now all you need to worry about is what song you're going to sing."

"You want me to sing?" My voice shot up a few octaves. "What are you talking about?"

He jerked his head to the left, and for the first time I noted a small makeshift stage with a microphone stand. Then he rose and moved to a portable closet. Inside, there were about a half dozen dresses and a pair of spiked boots. He grabbed a lacy black number and the boots, then carried them to me. "Change into these. You have five minutes before I return."

The dress and boots fell to the floor in front of me, and before I could inquire how I was supposed to do anything with my wrists bound, he snapped his fingers and disappeared. The manacles vanished right along with him.

I took a tiny moment to rub at my already raw wrists and hissed with pain. Instead of changing into someone else's clothes, I ran for the door but stopped in the middle of the room when I realized there wasn't a door at all.

"What the hell?" I cried as I ran to the wall, pressing against the smooth surface, looking for any crack or opening. Frantic, I moved along the panels, glancing up for an opening and checking the floor for some sort of access.

Nothing.

My breathing came fast, and I started to hyperventilate. How would anyone find me if there wasn't any way in?

"I'm here," a voice said from behind me.

I spun and let out a gasp of surprise. "Vienna."

"I'm sorry. You should never have been caught up in this." The ghost floated above the ground, wringing her hands.

"What are you… I mean, how are you here?" Her sudden appearance calmed me, and my panic subsided, especially since she was so coherent. All the other times I'd seen her on the ship, she'd either not noticed me or had been in a crazed state.

She shrugged. "We have some sort of connection. You can see me. No one else ever could, and it sort of drove me insane after a while."

Sort of insane? I didn't think sort of was quite the right description, but I kept that to myself.

"I tried every year to help Muse, but she could never see me or hear me. And now…" Her brows furrowed, and she frowned with worry shining in her eyes. "I don't know if she'll wake up."

My questions no longer seemed important. She had information I needed, and I wasn't about to let my curiosity derail her. "It's true then? What Xavier said? She's in a coma?"

She nodded. "Our only hope is your witch friend. She's trying to heal her. And while I wish I could help, no one can see me or hear me. Not even Razer." Pain flashed in her eyes at the mention of his name. "I don't know why. I think maybe Razer used too much energy trying to save Muse. I'll try later, try to let them know you're safe for now. But I had to make sure you were here first, and I want to help if I can."

"And where exactly are we?" I asked, glancing around at the desolate space.

"It's his chamber, but since it has no doors, no one knows exactly where it is. Not even me. I can will myself to be where you are, but I never know where that will be until I show up. It was the same with Muse."

I narrowed my eyes. He'd never get away with this crap. Not with me. Jade would find me and bust through his twisted magic in no time. Her or Julius.

She shook her head. "It's not that easy. His magic is strong. It's a curse that could kill—" Her voice broke on the word kill. She tightened her hands into fists as she went rigid with frustration. "We have to get you out of here before he curses you."

"I'm on board for that. What do you suggest?" I waved a hand around my doorless prison.

"You have to convince him you're not a threat. Don't give him any reason to spell you right away. If his history is any indicator, he'll want to banter with you before he spells you. Your best bet is to stall until I can reach Razer to let them know where you are."

"How long will that be?" The panic was building in my chest again. Vienna was a ghost, and not a very stable one at that. At least she hadn't been before. I wasn't sure I trusted her judgement.

"I don't know. We'll just have to wait it out—Oh no. He's coming. Remember what I said. Stall. Do what you have to." There was a crackle of magic in the air just as Vienna vanished.

Xavier reappeared, holding a large bottle of whiskey and a leather whip.

I backed up, holding my hands out. "Whoa. Hold on just a minute. No one ever said anything about whips." No one said anything about being holed up in a windowless room with a psycho either, but one problem at a time.

He set the whiskey down on the small round table and wrapped his hand around the whip, pulling it slowly over his skin as if savoring the sensation. "Don't worry about this, love. This is for me. Not you."

My stomach rolled. Of course it was for him, the sick bastard. I straightened my spine, glaring at him. "If you use that on me, I swear to the high heavens, I'll kill you with my bare hands."

His face flushed with pleasure as he let out a soft chuckle. "That's good. Tell me how you'd do it."

Oh for the love of... This guy was a real kinkster. He was enjoying my defiance entirely too much.

We stared at each other until the smile melted from his face and morphed into a sneer. "That's twice you've defied me. Once more and we're going to have an issue."

"Three strikes and I'm out?" I asked, my ire rising. "What then? You're going to reshackle me?" The moment the words were out of my mouth, dread set in. Why the heck had I reminded him I was free?

His gaze darted to the manacles hanging along the wall, then back to me. That slow, sinister smile spread over his face as he stood and moved toward me.

I stepped back and stumbled over the boots I'd never put on. I fell to one knee, catching myself before I sprawled across the floor.

He bent and picked up the dress. "I told you to change."

I said nothing as I stared up at his hardened expression and the three ragged scar lines marring his face. I hoped to hell

Muse had given him those.

"I left because I'm a gentleman. But it appears you can't be trusted to do as you're told."

Gentleman. Right. I snorted my disagreement. "Gentleman don't keep their guests locked up against their will."

"They do when their guests need to be punished."

Bile rose up in the back of my throat, and it was all I could do to keep from spitting on him. Punished. Just let him try. I eyed the whip now lying on the couch. If he got within five feet of me with that thing, he was going to find out exactly what pain meant. I had zero qualms about turning the tables on him. The first time he tried to whip me, I'd show him what it meant to be beaten.

He tossed the dress at me. "Since you can't obey, you'll now have to change in front of me."

I pushed myself to my feet and let the dress fall to the floor. "Then what?"

"Then we'll see how you stack up to Muse and Vienna." He backed up slowly, and when he reached the couch, he didn't take his eyes off me as he sat and grabbed the whip. He ran his hands over the braided cord as if it were a lover.

My stomach turned. "What if I refuse?"

"You won't." He sat back and propped one foot on his opposite knee.

His smug confidence made me long to clock him upside his pale head. I might've done it too if it weren't for Vienna's warning still playing in my mind. She's said to stall, to make sure he didn't spell me into submission. The immediate problem was he seemed to enjoy our verbal battle. How much was too much, and what if I pushed him too far?

I wasn't ready to give in just yet. If I was going to play this game, I had to know the limits. "You don't know anything about me."

That thin, almost white eyebrow of his rose again. "You think so? I know your name is Pyper Rayne. That you own a café in New Orleans but that your business partner, Kane Rouquette, owns the building. Your mother died shortly after you graduated college. Your father was an alcoholic; his whereabouts are unknown. He left one night after taking you to Dairy Queen to get your favorite ice cream. He just packed up and left. No good-byes, no promises, no contact."

I sucked in a sharp breath but said nothing.

His creepy smile widened. "You're a medium and are dating a man who recently got a new lease on life after being a ghost for almost a century." He stood, swishing the whip around in front of him as he strode toward me. "And my favorite fact. You put yourself through college as an exotic dancer."

Ice ran through my veins. Short of reciting my social security number and my limited list of actual boyfriends, he knew more about me than most of my friends did. But how? It wasn't as if I'd poured my heart out on an Internet blog. There was no point in denying it. He was far too spot-on to not have done his homework. "How do you know all that?"

"Let's just say it's my special gift." He reached down and grabbed the discarded dress. Holding it out to me, he said, "Take it."

My arm lifted, and my hand clutched the lacy fabric without any help from me. "What the—"

"Pick up the boots."

My lead feet shuffled forward until I was inches from the

leather boots. Then my knees bent, and even as I tried to stop myself, I reached for them.

"Good, Pyper. Now change."

"Stop!" I ordered even as I started tugging at my shirt. "Drop whatever spell you're using. I'll do as you ask."

He lowered himself onto the couch once more, pressing his lips into a thin line, contemplating me. "I think I prefer my way better."

I scowled, hating the way my fingers felt fat and clumsy under his spell. The truth was I didn't give a rat's butt about stripping in front of some strange guy. I wasn't modest. Not in the least. I was far more uncomfortable with the fact he'd stolen my free will.

"That's it," he urged when I stumbled out of my jeans. "Make sure you take it all off."

My hand immediately went to my bra hooks. Pure hatred consumed me. "You're a sick son of a bastard."

"There she is," he said, his eyes sparkling with humor. "Tell me what you're really thinking."

"That you're a sick pig who has to resort to curses in order to get a woman to show you her breasts. That once I'm finally free of this room and you, if Julius and Kane haven't already ended you, that I'm going to junk-punch you so hard your manbits will never work again."

"Bravo!" He clapped, beaming at me. "That was..." He sighed and pressed his hand to his heart. "Just what I was hoping for."

My fingers finally managed to get the clasps free, and I let out a curse as my bra snapped open. Before I flashed him all my goods, I crossed my arms over my chest, my glare daring the creepy perv to order me to continue to undress.

"Oh, let's save that reveal for later, shall we?" Xavier snapped his fingers.

Magic crackled over my skin, and suddenly I felt lighter, as if an invisible weight had been lifted off me. I quickly snapped my bra back into place and pulled the dress on.

"Slower," he ordered.

His words didn't force me to do anything, but I stilled my hands anyway. "Slower?"

"Yes. Take your time. I want to savor this." His voice had gone husky, as if he were talking to a lover.

I suppressed a shudder and did as he asked. Gliding my hand up my arm, I slid the strap of the dress over one shoulder and then the other one.

"Turn around." His breathing had quickened, and I had to fight the urge to hurl.

I still did as he asked and silently said a prayer that Vienna would hurry.

"Zip the dress up. Slowly."

I squeezed my eyes shut, inching the zipper up.

"What is going on in here?" a familiar shrill voice demanded.

My eyes flew open.

Ida May.

Relief flooded through me. I'd been found.

Chapter 20

"**Y**OU HAVE TO get out of here," Ida May said. "Julius is worried sick."

How, I mouthed, fearing that Xavier would hear me or somehow stop our exchange.

"I don't know. But strutting around for this pervert isn't the answer."

I wanted to scream. Had it really come to this? Putting my faith in Ida May, the ghost who'd spent most of her time talking about manbits and trying to hook up with other random ghosts whenever possible? I scowled at her. *You're not helpful.*

She lifted her hands in the air, palms up. "I just call 'em like I see 'em."

"Slip into the boots," Xavier said from behind me.

Get Julius. Or Jade, I mouthed to Ida May and then turned and made a show of lacing up the torturous stilettoed boots. My toes ached in the too-tight footwear.

"Perfect," he said, rubbing his hand over the back of his neck. "Now stand on the stage in front of the microphone."

I rose, and although I was normally an expert at walking in high heels, I stumbled across the small stage, my feet screaming in protest.

"You look like you're dressed up for Halloween. All you need is a pointed hat and a black cat." Ida May floated beside me, casting her glance up and down in judgement.

"Go away," I whispered through my teeth. "You're not helping."

"Geez. Touchy." She gave me an irritated look. "I was only trying to lighten the mood."

"If you want to help," I continued in a whisper, "find Julius and let him know where I am."

"I would, but I actually don't know where we are." She floated near the wall and flattened her hand against the metal. Instead of gliding right through like she normally would, her hand was blocked, effectively trapping her in. Just like me. She froze, her eyes filling with the same panic I'd been fighting off all evening.

"I'm trapped! What the hell? One minute I was promising Julius I'd look for you, and the next I was here. Now that pig has us both." She buried her hands into her dark unruly hair and started to spin around in a tizzy.

Son of a monkey! All my hopes of utilizing Ida May vanished. She was useless if she couldn't get word to Julius.

"What did you do to this room?" I yelled at Xavier, beyond caring what I might reveal of Ida May's presence. If he hadn't heard her or seen her yet, he likely couldn't at all. And since she was trapped too, she was hardly a threat to him.

He stopped fiddling with his music docking station and turned to stare at me. "Excuse me?"

I waved a hand around. "No doors. It's like a tin can. I'm sealed up in here. What kind of twisted person does this to someone?"

His face went blank, all humor gone. "It's only temporary, Ms. Rayne. You and your friends interrupted a sacred ritual that only happens once a year. Someone had to take Muse's place. And who better than the one who looks most like Vienna to fill her shoes?"

"What?" I clutched the microphone stand just to have something to hold on to. I didn't look anything like Vienna. She was elegant with long blond hair. I was petite, dark-haired, and alternative. "You mean Muse, right?"

He shook his head. "No. Vienna Vox. She was always experimenting with her look. I liked it best when she was goth. She was my soul mate, and once a year she put on a show just for me. Or she did until she started dating that dirty rocker."

The picture of Vienna with a shaved head flashed in my mind. That part of his story rang true. But a private show just for him? Had he hired her? Or had he spelled her like he had with Muse? How long had this twisted a-hole been living this fantasy?

His eyes crinkled with sadness. "Everything was fine until the dragon came along. If he hadn't—" He shook his head as if dislodging the thought. "Never mind. That's all old news. All you have to do is stay here with me for the next two days, then you're free to go."

Right. With a lovely spell that would keep me from talking about whatever we were going to do over the next thirty-six or so hours. And would I be required to come back to this ship every year for the rest of my life? No freakin' way. He was delusional if he thought my friends weren't going to bring him down.

Ida May floated across the room and hovered over him with

her hands fisted on her hips. "He's not very attractive is he?"

I had to fight back a startled, humorless laugh, not only because her comment was out of the blue, but because she was right. His eyes were too far apart, his ears slightly too big, and his shoulders had a permanent hunch. The scars on his face didn't help matters. But even so, if he'd been any sort of decent human being, all that could be considered interesting. Instead, all I saw was the ugliness of a selfish man who forced women to participate in his weird fetishes.

Ida May tapped a finger on her thigh. "I've seen plenty of his type before. The type that wouldn't have been welcome in the grand mansions in Storyville."

In other words, even if he had all the money in the world, he wouldn't have been welcome at the higher-class brothels on Basin Street. Just perfect. There was nothing to do but humor him, get as much information as possible so that once I was freed from this cage, we'd find a way to stop him for good.

"Why did you do it?" I asked.

He tilted his head to the side, curiosity replacing his blank expression. "Bring you here?"

"No. I've already figured that part out." Mostly. "I mean Vienna. If you loved her so much, why did you attack her?" What I really wanted to ask was why he'd thrown her overboard, but that might push him too far.

"That is none of your business." He sat up straight and leaned forward, peering at me. "How did you know about that?"

I shrugged, figuring there was no point in lying. "I'm a medium. I saw the echo of the altercation on the pool deck last night."

"You saw her?" There was longing in his tone now as he glanced around, a crazed look in his eyes. "Is she here now? Can you call her forth?"

"No. I just saw an echo," I reiterated, certain the last thing I wanted to do was let him believe I had any control over when she appeared and when she didn't. Who knew what he'd try to make me do then? "Like an imprint of a memory. Neither of you were actually there."

"Oh. I've seen her every now and then, but it never lasts. If I could just talk to her…" He stared past my shoulder, lost in thought.

The hair stood up on the back of my neck. The obvious disappointment in his tone gave me the creeps. This man had killed her, and yet he was desperate to connect with her again. He was one sick son of a bastard.

He reached over and pressed a button on his MP3 player. Slow, soulful music filled the room. His expressionless eyes met mine. "You will sing now."

A spark of energy skated over my skin, followed by the desire to hum a few lines of Vienna's most popular ballad. I gritted my teeth, knowing I'd been compelled to do just that.

Tightening my grip on the microphone, I swayed back and forth, letting the music move through me, and then opened my mouth, crooning, "Midnight, soft light, you're under my spell tonight."

"Oh no, Pyper! Stop." Ida May put her hands over her ears and gave me a look of sheer horror. "Don't ever do that again. Do you want fairies to die or something?"

I might have been compelled to sing, but Xavier's magic hadn't done anything to help my voice. I sucked in a breath and continued. "Candlelight, silent night, you're the one who makes everything all right."

The music stopped abruptly, followed by Xavier standing. He glared at me. "Are you singing like that on purpose?"

"If you are, it's sort of hilarious. If not, it's tragic. You should never sing." Ida May clamped a hand over her mouth, giggling.

I sighed. I'd always known singing wasn't exactly my calling, but I never imagined it was that terrible.

"Your voice isn't anything like Vienna's," Ida May pondered. "You'd be better off singing like Amy Winehouse. Sultry. Not soft and flowery."

She had a point, though I was miles from the soulful tone of the blues singer. Not that any of that mattered. Xavier wanted Vienna. Not an Amy impersonator. "No. I was a dancer. Not a singer."

Xavier's lips twisted into a snarl, then he reached over and slapped the play button on the MP3 player. "Do it again. Try harder this time. Let the music come from your soul. Make me *feel* it." He placed his hand over his heart and closed his eyes as if he were imagining how this was supposed to go. His eyes flew open, then narrowed. "Make me believe you. Otherwise your time here will come to an end. And it won't be pleasant."

Anger shot through my veins at his threat.

He glared at me, then started to pace. "I'm waiting."

"Well, he's a prickly pecker, isn't he?"

I turned my attention to Ida May, intending to tell her to shut it. Instead, I clamped my mouth shut when she started to sing Vienna's lyrics in a surprisingly delicate tone. Her voice was beautiful, breathtaking even.

She finished the first line of lyrics and winked at me. "Like that. Now it's your turn."

I shook my head, knowing I'd never sound like that.

"Sing!" Xavier ordered. "Put feeling into it, like you mean every word."

I cleared my throat.

Ida May hummed for a moment, then started to sing again. She stopped abruptly and in her own demanding tone said, "Do it with me."

Her sweet voice filled me as I closed my eyes and did my best to sing with her in harmony. It sounded better to my ears, but maybe it was just because I was hearing her. When we finally got to the end of the song, I opened my eyes and found Xavier leaning forward on the couch, still sneering at me.

"That was… I can't even express how awful it was. I was this close to stabbing myself in the ear." He got up and paced in front of me. "This isn't going to work."

I froze. What did that mean? Surely he wasn't going to let me go, not now that I knew who he was.

"You are worse than useless. Now you're a liability." He stomped around, tugging at his hair with both fists.

Liability. Crap on toast! That wasn't good.

"Say something!" Ida May urged. "Tell him you'll practice. Otherwise that psycho is going to feed you to the fishes."

I wanted to ignore her, but geez, she could be right.

He was mumbling to himself now and kicking at the couch.

I glanced at Ida May. She shot around the room, just as agitated as my captor. "Calm down!" I cried, not sure which one I was talking to.

They both froze.

Xavier recovered first. He squared his shoulders and moved toward me, determination in his focused gaze.

"Whoa!" I held my hands up. "There's no need to be hasty. I can try harder. Singing just isn't something I've done much of. I know if—"

He snaked his hand out and gripped my neck. Hard.

Can't breathe. Can't breathe. The words played over and over in my head as I clawed at his hand, trying and failing to dislodge his iron grip.

His eyes turned from dull blue to obsidian, and then he leaned in and kissed me.

Chapter 21

UNABLE TO MOVE and horrified to have the monster pressing his chapped lips to mine, I squeezed my eyes shut and tried to fade away into the back of my mind. To divorce myself from my current reality.

But then instead of kissing me, he loosened his hold on my neck just enough that he sucked the remaining air from my lungs. The deprivation sent me into instant panic. My lungs seized as I frantically tried to reclaim my air, and my limbs flailed, striking out at him with surprising force. Pain radiated up my arm when my fist slammed into his surprisingly solid chest.

He let out a grunt, immediately tightening his fingers around my neck. Blackness creeped in around the edges of my vision. This was it. He was going to kill me right there in the barren room. No last moments with Julius. No chance of fighting back. No one to witness my death except Ida May, my inappropriate ghost.

Heck, maybe we'd become BFFs in my afterlife. The idea took root and I vowed to haunt the crap out of Xavier. He'd rue the day he ever touched me. I'd sing in his ear, hide his keys, junk-punch him in his sleep.

Air rushed into my lungs along with a cooling sensation. Xavier pushed me back, and released me.

My legs collapsed under me, and I fell on the wooden stage, gasping for air.

"Pyper!" Ida May cried. I glanced up at her and watched as she screamed in his face. "You're a dead man. Touch her one more time and I'll make it my mission to turn you into swamp food. Stupid, no-good piece of beetle dung."

He didn't even flinch. Of course he didn't. He couldn't hear her threats. "Get up," he ordered.

My legs curled under me and I rose automatically. I stared at my limbs, hating the way my body responded to him against my will. "Is that what that *kiss* was about? Spelling me?"

He tapped the MP3 player once more. The music to another one of Vienna's most popular songs filled the room. "Sing."

Her words belted from my lips, sounding deeper and raspier than hers ever did, but my tone was infinitely better than it had been before.

The frustrated lines around his eyes smoothed out as he relaxed back into the couch.

As the music faded, my voice trailed off and silence filled the room.

"Holy balls," Ida May finally said. "If he spelled you permanently, you could take that show on the road."

I grimaced. Being spelled, or more likely cursed, was repugnant. My skin crawled just thinking about it.

"Stop scowling," Xavier said, his tone cold. "The next time, act like you mean it. Move those hips and feel the lyrics. I want you to seduce me with the music."

My stomach turned.

"Jeez. What a freak." Ida May moved away from him as if even hovering near him would give her cooties. "I have got to get out of here."

"You?" I said and immediately regretted it when Xavier turned in her direction.

"Who are you speaking to?"

The heat rose in the room a few degrees, and the lights seemed to dim slightly. I blinked and felt a profound sense of loss when I realized Ida May had vanished. It wasn't as if she'd been all that helpful, but at least with her around, I'd felt less... alone.

"Tell him it's me," Vienna said from beside me.

I started and took a step away from her. When had she gotten there?

"It's your only hope," she added, already moving toward him.

"Ms. Rayne, speak."

There was no holding back, not when he gave me a direct order, thanks to his curse. "Vienna is here."

His jaw tightened and he glared at me. "Do not lie to me."

I cut my gaze to Vienna. She stood right next to him, a scary look on her normally angelic face. "I'm not lying. She's here. To your left."

She turned and met my eyes, fire burning in her gaze. "Tell him I want him to let you go."

Xavier stiffened and reached out to Vienna, his hand going right through her transparent body.

She shivered, but her voice remained strong. "Tell him."

I swallowed, certain this wouldn't go well. "She wants you to let me go."

His head snapped toward me. "I think you understand that isn't going to happen."

Vienna lifted into the air, and her body started to glow.

I sucked in a sharp breath when he lifted his head in her direction.

"She's there isn't she?" he asked.

"Can you see her?" My heart sped up and my skin prickled as nervousness shot through me. Something was about to happen, but I didn't know what.

He shook his head. "I... feel her," he said breathlessly, his face lighting up with incandescent lust.

Something inside me died. This man had killed her because of his obsession. And with that realization my knees nearly buckled as I sank to the floor. How long had I been in this room? Hours? Was there really any chance he was going to let me go? I wasn't Muse. And I knew what he'd done to her. My only hope was that he'd spell me to keep silent, but he had to realize I had powerful friends. Unless he was a complete idiot, I was likely to end up just like Vienna.

"I'm going to stop him," Vienna said.

"How?" I asked, no longer caring what Xavier heard.

"How what?" he asked.

I ignored him as I sat on the stage, my head in my hands.

"Trust me." She left Xavier and moved to hover near me.

"Were you talking to her?" Xavier whispered, cocking his head to the side as if listening for her.

I stifled a groan.

"Answer me!"

"Yes." The word flew out of my mouth, but I clamped my lips shut, determined to not say any more than I had to.

"What did she say? Is she here to see me?" The hopefulness radiating from him made me want to hurl.

"Don't answer that!" Vienna cried, but the words were already on the tip of my tongue. "No!"

She barreled into me, her ghost-self dousing me in ice water. "Hey!" I cried out.

Don't fight it, Vienna said in my head.

"What the—" My words cut off even though my lips were still moving. No sound, no words, no nothing. I was mute.

Relax, Vienna said. *I'm visiting your body. I'm here to help you get out of this mess.*

How? I'm not a witch. You shouldn't be able to share my space like this. Hadn't we determined Razer had invaded Julius because they both had magic?

You do have magic. A faint trace of it. I can feel it in your blood. Just enough to make a difference. That, along with the fact that you're a medium, is enough.

Her words shocked me into silence. Magic? Me? How was that possible? *No. You're wrong. I don't have magic.*

Think about it, Pyper. Haven't you ever done something you can't explain? Something you brushed off as something else?

The recent memory of shouting at the same time the spell was neutralized in room 1538 flashed in my mind. But that was a coincidence, wasn't it?

No. It wasn't. Your magic isn't strong. Probably not something you'd ever notice. But it's enough to make a difference when you're working with someone else. Now work with me so we can defeat this creep.

Her words gave me hope, but I was still skeptical. What if our souls merged? Panic raced up my spine. I'd been here before, and even though I was sure she was trying to help, I'd almost rather take my chances with the perverted man-witch than risk losing my soul.

Trust me. It was Jade's idea.

Jade? You spoke to her? Relief washed through me at the thought. She wouldn't rest until she found me. Neither would Kane or Julius.

No. But I did talk to Razer. This is the current plan. If you let me in, we can fight this bastard with my magic and save us both.

Save us both. Her words echoed in my mind, and all my resistance vanished. My limbs relaxed. My breathing evened out. And then I felt light, airy, as if I were floating.

"Vienna?" Xavier asked, his eyes wide.

I stared down at myself, or tried to, but my gaze was fixated on Xavier, Vienna's hatred filling every corner of my soul.

"Xavier," Vienna said. "It's been a long time."

"Ten years." He reached for her hand, and to my surprise, she let him take it.

The sensation was extremely weird and totally foreign. I could sense him touching my hand, but at the same time, I had the feeling that I was living in a dream—present, but not.

His fingers laced through hers. Every muscle in my body stiffened, but Vienna's tone was careful, devoid of any anger. "Is there somewhere we could go to talk?" She glanced around the stark room. "Somewhere that doesn't feel like a dungeon."

He tightened his grip on my hand and frowned. "But this is the safest place. No one will bother us here."

"There's no window. I want to see the ocean, feel the sea air as we reconnect." The disgust she churned up as she sweet-talked him stayed in a tightly coiled ball in my stomach. Her acting skills and self-control were off the chart.

Xavier gazed at her like a lovesick puppy. He reached up and brushed the hair behind my ear, trailing his fingers down my jawline. "You know we can't do that, love."

Ugh. How was she just standing there, letting him place his hand on me? If I'd been in possession of my body, I'd have broken a finger or five. That is until he ordered me to be the good little obedient singer.

"You have the power to keep everyone away. Look at everything you've accomplished. You fought Razer and won. You kept Muse from spilling your secrets. And if our fight hadn't been so passionate, I'm sure we'd have found a way to be together. You're stronger than this. Xavier. Let's find a way out of this room and into the sun, where we can begin again."

A small smile turned the corner of his lips up as he let his gaze wander the length of my body. "You have no idea how much I've longed to hear you say those words. I'm sorry, Vee. I never meant to hurt you." He leaned in, pressing his forehead to mine.

"I know," she said softly, but inside, her emotions were a turbulent storm. Blood rushed through my veins, followed by something electric, something powerful, something so strong my insides vibrated with it.

Her magic.

It filled me up, consumed me, made me itch to use it.

Relax, she ordered in my mind. *This is what is going to save you once he releases us from this room. If you try to syphon the magic from me, we're both going to suffer.*

I had no idea what she meant by both of us. She was a ghost and presumably could leave anytime she wanted. But if she was right and I stole her magic from her somehow, it wasn't likely I'd escape the command spell he'd put on me. And since I'd had no idea how to wield magic anyway, I did as she asked, trying my damnedest to not interfere.

"Come," Xavier said, tugging her toward the couch. "Sit with me for a minute."

She hesitated.

Xavier's eyes narrowed. "I said come."

The spell he'd put on me flared to life, and everything in me ached to do as he said.

But that wasn't the case for Vienna. She held the spell back, keeping her free will.

I wanted to do a fist pump and cheer her on. There was nothing better than a strong, clever woman beating back a small, entitled man who thought he could use people and take whatever he wanted. She... no, *we* were going to make this douche-bucket pay for his sins. Just as soon as we got an opening. She might have the magic, but I had the body, and we needed to work together to end this loser.

Do what he says, I said. *Make him think he still has the upper hand. He'll never leave this place if he doesn't think he has control.*

Her resistance instantly vanished and she nodded at Xavier. "Of course. Anything you want."

The tension in his shoulders eased slightly as he smiled at her, but made no move to pull me onto the couch. Instead, he wrapped an arm around my waist, tugging me in close to his rail-thin body.

She let him, even tucked my head against his knobby shoulder. He smelled of mothballs and stale coffee. The stench burned my nostrils, and I longed for the rich aroma of the mocha lattes I served back at the café.

You'll be there soon enough, Vienna said. *All I need is for him to release us from this room. Then all hell is going to break loose.*

Chapter 22

XAVIER HUGGED ME to his side, his grip strong and biting into my upper arm.

Vienna just gazed up at him, ignoring the pain I knew she had to be feeling. "Please, Xav? I'm ready to start fresh."

He tilted his head to the side and studied her. "What about Ms. Rayne? She's still with you, right? We'll need to do something about her."

"Yes, she's here, but I'm a witch. I'm stronger than her. She has no hope of taking over, and before long, she'll fade away entirely. It'll just be you and me... forever."

Her words about me fading away rang true. It was nearly impossible for two souls to share the same body for very long before one took over. Was she playing me? Was all of this to get a new lease on life? How far was she willing to go after her decade-long ordeal?

It didn't matter. I didn't have a choice. She had control over me. And if we escaped this dungeon, my chances of survival were infinitely better.

"You do seem to be getting stronger by the minute." He lifted a lock of my normally black hair so it was in my sight. Only it wasn't black, it was blond. Blond with copper streaks in it. Vienna's hair.

Holy crow, even my appearance was being taken over.

"It's because of you," she whispered in his ear. "You have given me the strength to come back, to fight for what I want. But I want to be equals this time. Can we do that? Start over? Become the couple you always wanted us to be? Razer is gone. So are the pressures of my career. I can sing for you and only you."

"Only me?" He stood up straighter, his shoulders back, preening like a freakin' peacock. "But what if I want to show you off?"

She forced a smile. "We can make that happen. But not until I give you your private show." Pressing her palm to his chest, she rose onto her tiptoes and kissed him.

Full-on kissed him, tongue warring with his, my body pressed against his, my other hand gripping his hip.

He twisted, burying his hand in her hair, grinding against me, his mouth working like a starving man.

I recoiled in the back of my mind, distancing myself from the violation. She might have taken over my will, but I still felt everything. Had to be witness to her fierce determination to do whatever it took to end him. His greedy mouth claiming mine, his rough hands manhandling me as if he had a right to my body.

The urge to unleash the power still flowing through my veins, to fry him with it, to watch him burn, pushed every other thought out of my mind. I craved revenge. Was consumed with hatred. Was ready to finish him.

He broke away, pushing Vienna back as he gasped for breath and held his hands up. "Not like this. Not here."

"I want you now. I want my hands on you. And you begging me for mercy." She took a step forward, her voice husky with what appeared to be lust. And it was. Bloodlust. As soon as she had her opportunity, she was going to kill him.

I was going to be used to kill him.

Horror filled me. *No!* I cried. *We can't do that. We have to turn him over to the Witches' Council. They'll take care of him. They'll decide his punishment.*

It wasn't that I didn't want to see him pay for his crimes. There was no doubt he deserved it. But I wasn't prepared to be involved in ending someone's life. I wasn't the judge and jury, even if she had good reason to be.

Vienna didn't respond to my outburst. Instead, she called up more power, the magic swirling like a hurricane force beneath my skin.

"You'll be the one doing the begging, Vienna," he said, all traces of seduction gone from his tone. "No one plays me."

Magic shot from his fingertips at the same time Vienna raised my hand and her magic exploded into an invisible wall. The moment his spell hit, the wall shattered into a million pieces.

Holy hell. All bets were off. I had no idea how he knew she was lying, but it was clear he hadn't bought a word of her act.

Xavier leaped forward, both hands stretched out, reaching for my neck. Vienna rolled off the small stage, shooting a stream of magic right at him. Her feet landed on the floor as her magic hit him squarely in the chest, propelling him across the room. He slammed into the wall and, as if in slow motion, slid down to the floor.

Whoa. You're badass, I said to Vienna.

A ripple of her pleasure fluttered through me at my compliment. She stalked across the room to her murderer and crouched down in front of him. He had a blank expression on his dazed face, but with one touch of her hand to his neck, he blinked and recognition dawned.

"You're going to pay for this… again," he growled.

"I doubt it. I'm not that naïve witch anymore, taken off guard by your subtle spells and potions. You're the worst kind of predator. The kind that people look past because you're a nice guy. The kind no one believes is a monster. But I know better. I know those herbs you gave me left me impaired and unable to fight you off. You're a coward, pathetic, and deserve to rot in hell."

"You first." Magic crackled around us as they both struck at the same time. Vienna's was pure white magic, not unlike Jade's, while Xavier's had a dark gray tint, laced with black magic.

Watch out! I cried when he shot something that looked like a fireball at us. Vienna dropped to her knee, barely avoiding the attack.

But Xavier was too quick, already mumbling something as pure black energy rose around him, swirling like a cape. His body shimmered, going transparent as he started to fade away.

"Oh no you don't!" Vienna jumped to her feet. "You're not going anywhere without me." She raised her arms and shouted, "*Iunctio!*"

The black magic shot from Xavier and encircled us. His eyes darkened once again to obsidian as his lips twisted into a sinister snarl.

"You're not getting away with anything this time," Vienna

said, her tone so calm and icy cold that a dread settled in my gut.

What did that mean?

The blank walls of the dungeon melted away, replaced by mirrored walls, plush carpeting, and bright light streaming through a large window.

"Idiot," Xavier said and reached for Vienna.

She stepped back, or tried to, but was frozen in place. "What the—"

"You didn't think I was going to let you hitch a ride and escape just like that, did you?" he asked, anger making his voice shake. His long limbs were jerky as he reached for her again.

I recoiled, still shunted to the background inside my own body. Vienna's fear and panic mixed with my own, and that's when I started to worry.

You have to stop him, I said.

"I... can't." She was frozen. Locked in place. His magic had done something to her, neutralized her. Made it so she couldn't fight back once again.

His hands closed around her throat, squeezing until she choked.

My own consciousness faded in and out as he dragged my body toward the blinding sunlight.

"You can't be trusted. I always knew you were a liar." The hatred and disappointment emanating from him startled me. The entire time we'd been in his prison, he'd shown affection, even his twisted form of love for her. Now his true colors had shown themselves. This is what he'd been like the night he'd thrown her over the railing ten years ago. The desperate man who couldn't live with the fact that she would never love him.

And now it was even worse. She'd made him think, even if only for a few moments, that she was willing to give him everything he ever wanted. But she'd betrayed him, and he was going to make her pay.

Make me pay.

The sliding glass door opened with an ear-piercing screech.

"It should never have come to this," Xavier whispered into my ear, his breath hot and smelling of rotten eggs.

I recoiled, flinching in his arms, and let out a tiny gasp of air when I realized Vienna was no longer in charge of my body. I glanced down at my pale skin, noted the silver ring I wore on my right ring finger and my electric-blue nail polish.

Xavier's hand tightened around my neck, followed by the other one, yanking on my hair, snapping my head back. He stared into my eyes, his changing from obsidian back to pale, lifeless blue. "Where did she go?" Xavier demanded, shaking me. "We weren't done here."

I tried to shake my head but couldn't. He had me locked in place. I struggled to suck in air, resulting in a sick, gurgling noise as my vision started to blur again. If I didn't get free, I was going to pass out any second. I had to do something.

Anything.

"That stupid witch." Xavier pushed me toward the railing, slamming my back against the metal bars. "You in there, Vienna?"

Was she? I had no idea. And no idea how to answer. So I went with my gut and choked out, "No, she isn't."

"Son of a—"

I kicked out. Hard. My boot struck his shin. He let out a surprised grunt and lost his balance, causing him to release his hold just enough that I was able to pull away from his death grip.

"You stupid—"

The refresher self-defense class I'd taken less than a week ago sent me into overdrive. Using the heel of my hand, I thrust upward, catching his nose, and jerked my knee forward, ramming him in the groin.

Only he dodged to the left and my knee hit his thigh instead, but that didn't save his nose. A sickening crack rang in my ears, followed by blood gushing down his face.

His hand clasped over my forearm just as I spun, catching him with a roundhouse kick to the side of the head. He released his grip and slammed into the side of the railing, his body folding in on itself.

Finish him, Vienna said, apparently still sharing my body. *Don't let him do this to anyone else. Throw him overboard, just like he did to me.* Vienna's words mixed with my adrenaline and I took a step forward, more than willing to do her bidding.

Xavier was still crumpled on the balcony, blood dripping from his nose when I yanked on his hair, forcing him to look up at me.

Hatred stared back at me.

I didn't care. There was a force inside me now, willing and ready to end him. Power so sweet, so all-encompassing, radiated down to my fingertips. Vienna's power.

Use it. Do what you have to, she urged.

I wanted to. Ached to do it. To send him over the rail of the ship. To make him suffer just as Vienna had.

"You don't have the nerve," Xavier spat.

"Watch me." Her power crackled down my arms.

"Release the magic," Xavier ordered, lumbering to his feet, confidence in his smug expression.

Only his commands didn't work on me anymore. Nothing he said had any hold on me. The fight, Vienna's magic, whatever it was, had completely broken his spell. He didn't know it yet, but his curse had been neutralized. I raised my arms, shooting a stream of magic right at his chest. It smacked into him, contorting his body as the electric current rippled through him.

He screamed, and his black magic billowed from his palms into a cloud, slowly moving toward me.

I stood my ground, Vienna's desire for revenge and my need for justice merging into one thought—Xavier was finished. Her magic crackled at my fingertips, the intoxicating strength of it making me feel invincible.

Bloodlust. It was right there, consuming me. Everything narrowed around me, and all I saw was Xavier, his lanky body hunched over, dull blue eyes locked on mine, evil lurking beneath the surface. Hatred coiled inside me, for what he'd done to her, to Muse, and to me. For any other woman he'd put through hell to feed his twisted desires.

"You're done." I took a step forward, lifted my arms, and unleashed the torrent of magic. Dark gray light shot from my palms, colliding with his black cloud. The two streams mixed, then suddenly erupted into a blazing ball of fire. The explosion knocked me back into the suite, and I landed with a muffled thump.

That dark gray magic coiled around me, the heat of it nearly burning my skin.

Again! Vienna ordered.

I shook my head, my body trembling as I finally registered what was happening.

Dark gray magic meant one thing—her magic was tainted with evil.

Chapter 23

XAVIER STORMED INTO the room, small burn holes in his clothes, and smoke clinging to him. The charred smell of hair filled my senses, nearly making me gag.

"Get up!" he ordered.

I did as I was told, but only because being sprawled on the ground wasn't going to do me any favors with a pissed-off witch coming for me.

"You're going to need to do a lot more damage than that if you expect to take me down."

I stood there, frozen with indecision as Vienna's power strummed through me, ready for the taking. Deep down, I knew she was tapping into something far too dark. I'd been around Jade and the coven long enough to know what black magic could do to a person. Add the fact that I wasn't a witch, was a complete novice at using magic, and utilizing her power was a really bad idea. I could end up going insane from the evil magic, or worse. A shuddering chill ran through me. I was in a lose-lose situation.

I had no choice.

If I didn't use my only viable weapon, Xavier would take Vienna and me down. With a heavy heart, I took one step forward, meeting Xavier head-on, and unleashed her poisonous power.

Xavier snarled and met my attack with one of his own. The two magic streams collided once again, only this time instead of an explosion, something deep inside me snapped. I felt giant, unstoppable, invincible. Nothing could beat me, least of all Xavier.

The magic pouring from me curled in on itself and formed a giant dragon. The black-and-silver creature took flight, diving headfirst into the black magic. His mighty jaws opened, and I half expected him to breathe fire. Instead, he sucked in Xavier's stream of magic, shielding Vienna and me.

Xavier's eyes widened and his mouth fell open as he tried to back up, but he couldn't. He was locked in place, joined with my magical dragon.

How are you doing that? Vienna's voice was back, full of awe.

Me? I shot back. *No idea. Is your spirit animal a dragon or something?*

No. I don't have one.

Neither do I. But it appeared I did now, at least for the moment. The dragon continued to steal Xavier's magic, the creature growing with each passing moment while Xavier fell to one knee, barely hanging on.

His face had turned gaunt and his skin waxy with exhaustion.

I redoubled my efforts, pouring more magic into the dragon, urging him to drain the witch, to take every last bit of his magic until he was weak and begging for mercy.

The vindictiveness started as a small ball of hatred and quickly grew, snowballing at an alarming rate.

Yes, Vienna urged, cheering me on.

I ignored her, so consumed by the need to end the man now kneeling in front of me.

"You'll never hurt anyone again," I said, my voice gravelly to my own ears.

His eyes glazed over and his mouth worked, but no words came out.

The dragon's silver scales turned jet-black, and his eyes glowed red as the last dregs of magic slipped from the man. Xavier fell forward, landing on his hands and knees, frail and broken, completely neutralized.

"Look at me," I ordered.

His head slowly rose, shaking from the effort. His pale blue eyes were now ash gray, empty, soulless.

I didn't care. His time was up. Never again would he lay a hand on another innocent woman. "Good-bye, Xavier," I said so calmly my voice was foreign even to my own ears.

His eyes closed and he hung his head, prepared for his sentence.

Elation strummed through my veins, energizing me as I focused on my dragon. His head turned to the side, his glowing red eye locking with my gaze. Silent communication passed between us, and then I nodded once and unleashed my dragon.

He shot to the ceiling, hovering directly over Xavier, his black scales outlined with shimmering silver.

Time seemed to stand still in that moment as I saw exactly what would happen to the witch. The dragon would unleash his fire, blasting Xavier with magic so dark it would reduce him to ashes.

Icy fear crawled up my spine and my breath got caught in

my throat. I'd ordered this. And I couldn't stop it. Not now. The dragon was no longer within my control. He was now in possession of all the power I'd taken from both Vienna and Xavier.

I wasn't sure how I'd done it, but I'd created a literal monster filled with black magic.

The dragon's jaws opened, and a torrent of evil came gushing out, instantly incinerating the light fixture mounted to the ceiling. Silver flecks of metal rained down in the following silence.

Holy heavens, Vienna said, her fear seeping into mine. *What have we done?*

There was no time to answer. The dragon shifted suddenly, spinning and wrapping his tail around himself right before he dove straight for Xavier.

"No!" I cried, horrified.

The door slammed open, and familiar voices filled the room, shouting orders and incantations.

Strong arms wrapped around me, yanking me away from Xavier and the now-snarling dragon. My breath came in short gasps and tears stung my eyes as I realized the strong arms belonged to Julius.

"Are you okay? Are you hurt?" he asked, setting me on my feet near the door.

"I'm all right," I forced out, grasping his arm as I watched Jade cast a giant white net of magic over the dragon. His wings flapped sporadically, and smoke poured from his nostrils. She stepped back, pulling her net and the dragon away from Xavier.

Kane stood to the side of her, his demon-hunter amulet out, the eye trained on the murderer. If he even flinched, Kane would take him down.

Julius tightened his hold on me for just a moment, then released me. Staring me in the eye, he said, "I'm going to help Jade. Do not move."

I nodded once, but as soon as he released me, I backed up until I ran into the wall. My knees buckled and I slid to the floor, my hands shaking. The reality of what had almost happened hit me hard. My vision blurred and the room began to spin. Pain shot through my temple, and I grabbed the sides of my head, rocking back and forth as my stomach rolled.

"Pyper?" The voice was familiar but I couldn't place it.

The pain intensified. Everything pulsed inside me, needles stabbing my insides, heat burning me from the inside out.

"Pyper!" The cry was more frantic now.

I lifted my gaze and wasn't surprised to see the dragon had freed himself from Jade's net. He was right in front of me, his glowing red eyes studying me. Silver magic crackled over his black scales. We locked gazes, and everything else fell away. All that existed in that moment were me and the black-magic dragon. His glowing red eyes bored into mine. Revenge. Hatred. Evil. It was all right there at the surface, giving the dragon life.

And he was a part of me. We were connected. Had the same goal. Without him, I was nothing.

Shaking, I lifted my arm and reached out, needing to once again feel the magic he now carried. My fingers trembled with anticipation. The need consumed me. There was nothing I needed more than the magic. I climbed to my feet, straining to reach him.

And then, just before my fingers brushed his shimmering

scales, a deafening blast shot from across the room.

The dragon exploded into a million tiny little pieces, his shimmering scales twinkling in the afternoon sunlight.

Then I started to scream.

✧　✧　✧

Everything hurt. Muscles ached. My eyes watered. And the silence was deafening in the dark room.

I turned my head, wincing at the pain that shot down my shoulder and the ice pick slamming into my brain.

"Oh son of a—" I clamped my mouth shut, trying and failing to swallow. My throat was too raw, too dry. Water. I needed water.

Reaching out, I ran my hand over a hard, cool surface near the bed. Nothing.

Too weak to call out or to stand, I rolled onto my side and curled into the fetal position, squeezing my eyes shut again.

✧　✧　✧

"You don't have to do this," a female voice said.

"Aye, I do. What happened the other night…" Bootlegger's voice trailed off.

My eyes popped open. I blinked and rubbed the sleep from my eyes, noting the pale morning light creeping in through the window.

"Come on. You didn't do anything. Not really. Pyper stopped you before things went too far." The female sounded suspiciously like Ida May.

My body felt heavy, almost weighted down as I tried to push myself up.

"Wha' happens next time I lose my mind?" The pirate ghost floated back and forth as if he was pacing.

"You don't have to stay here. Come back to New Orleans. The shop is on Bourbon Street." She gave him a knowing smile and slipped into a seductive tone. "I'm there, and the party never stops."

A spark of interest lit his expression in the early-morning light, but then he shook his head, scowling at her. "No. I'm not interested in living like that no more."

She gave him a flat stare. "Please. You're a pirate. As long as you don't go possessing anyone else—"

I cleared my throat, barely getting the sound out through the dry passageway. Cripes, I needed water.

"Pyper?" Ida May's shrill voice filled the room. "You're awake!"

I nodded and turned my attention to the nightstand, nearly crying in relief when I spotted the glass of water.

"I have to get Julius," she cried, and with a little pop she disappeared from the room.

The cool water hit my throat, and I nearly cried with relief. After gulping down the entire glass, I slumped back against the pillows, already exhausted from the effort. My body was still stiff and everything ached, but at least my head was clear and I was awake.

How long had I been passed out?

I glanced around the room, noting I was back in the cabin I'd been sharing with Julius... and so was Bootlegger. He hovered in the corner, staring out the window as if he was deep in thought.

"What don't you have to do?" I asked, recalling Ida May's

words.

He turned to me, his expression haunted. "Leave this realm."

I furrowed my brows. "What do you mean?"

His jaw tightened and he clenched his fists at his sides. "I saw you. Saw that bastard controllin' you." He glanced away, once again staring out at the sea. "It opened my eyes, and now I know I have no honor. Invading someone for my own pleasure…"

Whoa, whoa, whoa. He *saw* me? "When?"

His head swiveled in my direction. "When what?"

"When did you see me?"

His expression turned to one of disgust. "When you were in that magical room. Ida May asked me for help to find it. I did, finally, but there was a barrier keepin' me out. Ida May too. We could see through the veil but couldn't reach you."

"But Ida May was there. I saw her. Heard her."

"She doesn't know how she got there or why she was cast out. It was after she saw you that she asked me to help. Your friends and lover were frantic with worry, searchin' the entire ship. But his dungeon was hidden with magic. They were never going to find you."

"And how did you find it?" I was hungry for information now.

His lips twitched with a hint of amusement. "Ma'am, I've been hauntin' this ship for many years. There isn't an inch o' this place I'm not on intimate terms with."

Of course there wasn't. I sat back against the headboard, clutching at the covers. I was fully dressed, but sitting in bed having a conversation with a ghost was a little unnerving. Even if I was a medium.

I wanted to ask how they'd found us in the suite, but my vision was going blurry again and the room started to spin.

Madeline wants to talk to you, Vienna said in my mind.

I sucked in a sharp breath, startled I was still merged with the ghost. The increased intake of oxygen cleared my head and vision.

She's hovering near the door.

Irritation flared deep inside me. "Give me a break, will you? Whatever that was that happened with your magic, it left me feeling like I was run over by a truck."

"What?" Bootlegger asked.

"Not you. Vienna."

He glanced around the room and frowned. "I don't see her."

"I know."

Sorry, Vienna said, her irritation mixing with mine. *Was only trying to help.*

My skin started to itch and I fidgeted, wishing I knew how to dispel her.

Her irritation vanished and a strange peace settled over me. *I'll leave when the time is right.*

I swung my feet over the side of the bed, and although my muscles were stiff, I was able to stand, all traces of dizziness gone. Tilting my head, I gazed at the door and waited. After a moment, I spotted a slim woman wearing a blood-red bustled dress with intricate black lace trim. Her wavy blond hair was piled high on her head, and her neck was accented with a black pearl choker. She moved toward me, a quiet smile claiming her lips.

"Hello," I said, meeting her smile with one of my own. "Are you here to talk to me?"

She nodded. "Yes. It's about Elias."

I eyed the soft-spoken ghost. "Elias?"

"Madeline?" Bootlegger's voice was soft and full of awe.

I glanced between the two ghosts. "You know each other?"

"Madeline!" Bootlegger rushed over to the woman, his eyes bright with emotion.

She laughed as she held a hand out to him. "It's been a long time, hasn't it?"

He swept her up in his arms and twirled her. When he finally stopped, he held her at arm's length and stared her in the eye. "Where have you been all these years? I searched and searched, but—"

"I've been waiting for you." She pressed a delicate hand to his hardened face. "Waiting for you to understand."

I watched the two of them, my heart nearly exploding from the tenderness of the moment. Who would've ever thought salty old Bootlegger with his crusty attitude would've been connected with the lovely creature standing in front of me.

He let her go and took a step back. "Understand what?"

She lowered her long dark lashes for a moment, then shyly met his gaze, her eyes soft. "Love."

He shook his head, his frown deepening. "I know how to love. I loved you every day of the twelve years we knew each other."

She nodded. "I know, Elias. That's why I waited. But you needed to learn to love others and, more importantly, yourself before we could spend eternity together."

The irritation drained from his face, replaced by wonder as

he watched her. "Eternity."

She moved toward him, her hands pressing against his chest. "Yes. Eternity. But you have to do something for me first."

"Anything." The word came out in a rush, breathless.

"You have to find a way to make things right with the young man you possessed the other night. Your actions cost him his fiancée."

"I... dammit." He hung his head.

"When it's done, I'll be back." Madeline pressed her fingertips to her lips, then to his. And as they stood there staring at each other, she faded away.

His head snapped up, and his eyes met mine. "I need your help."

My heart was full after witnessing them together. I'd never have guessed Bootlegger was anything more than a pilfering pirate. But it had all been an act. Just a way to forget what he'd once had and lost. "It would be my pleasure."

He nodded once. "Thank you. I'll be at the Green Parrot when you're ready." Without waiting for my reply, he glided through the wall, disappearing from the room.

The door slammed open, followed by Jade and Kane rushing in.

"Pyper!" Jade cried and wrapped her arms around me. "You're okay."

Kane beamed at me from over her shoulder. "Hey, Pypes. Looks like you kicked some major witch ass."

Tears burned my eyes as I hugged Jade and smiled at my best friend. "I couldn't have done it without you guys."

Jade pulled back, holding my shoulders with her hands, and studied me. "You're okay, really?"

I nodded. "Now I am." But my smile faded. "Where's Julius?"

"Dealing with the Witches' Council. The ship is docking later this morning. He's making arrangements for the enforcer to pick up Xavier. He'll be here in a few minutes."

I sat down heavily on the bed, a wave of fatigue rolling over me.

"Pyper?" Jade said, slipping her hand into Kane's. Her fingers tightened until they were almost white.

"What is it?" I asked, suddenly alarmed.

"It's Muse. She needs your help."

"Mine? Is she awake? Seeing spirits?"

Jade shook her head. "No, she's still unconscious. And the only way to reverse the spell Xavier used on her is with his magic."

My heart started to pound against my ribcage. If I never saw that bastard again it would be too soon. "Okay, but I don't see what that has to do with me. Can't you or the council force him to do whatever it is she needs?"

"I wish we could." Jade glanced up at Kane, her eyes pleading with him.

He let out a long breath, released her hand, and came to sit next to me.

I leaned into him. "Just tell me. Whatever it is, I'm sure I can take it."

"You incapacitated Xavier. He doesn't have any more magic. You're Muse's only hope."

My eyes widened as fear settled over me. The last thing I wanted to do was deal with magic again, especially magic I didn't know how to control. And to have a woman's life depending on me… "You mean I have to reverse the spell on her?"

Kane gave me a small nod. "I'm afraid so."

Chapter 24

MUSE LAY ON her bed, perfectly still. Her pale face was ashen in the midmorning light, and if Jade hadn't assured me she was still breathing, I'd have sworn we'd already lost her.

"Xavier's spell did this?" I asked Jade, sitting on the edge of her bed in the oversized stateroom. Because Muse was part of the band, she had a nicer room than the rest of us.

Jade nodded, her expression solemn. "It's black magic, and the only way I know to reverse it is by using the witch's magic that cast the spell. Xavier's. But his has been neutralized. And I have a strong suspicion you were the one who did it."

"Not me." I wrapped my hand around Muse's lifeless fingers, feeling a kinship to the woman who'd been under Xavier's spell for the past decade. "It was Vienna."

"Vienna?" Jade clasped a hand over her mouth. Then she shook her head. "Xavier was telling the truth then."

"If he said Vienna possessed me, then he's mostly right." I grimaced. "She's on board, so to speak, just like Razer is with Julius." A pang of Vienna's sadness mixed with my anxiousness at the mention of our significant others. Julius was still dealing with the council, and I'd yet to see him since I'd rejoined the living.

Jade closed her eyes and touched my arm, her brow furrowed in concentration. After a moment she let out a sigh of relief. "Two separate strands of energy. No soul merging. Thank the gods."

"Not yet anyway," I said, almost too afraid to believe her.

Xavier's in custody. Why are you still hanging around? I asked Vienna.

There's still work to do, she said stubbornly. *I'm not going anywhere until I'm certain everyone is safe.*

Everyone. What exactly did that mean? Muse and Razer? The entire ship? Anyone in danger from creepy perverts? Just how long was I going to be a conduit for the witch? At least I was in charge… for now.

I turned to Jade. "What is it you want me to do?"

"Well, I need to reverse the spell from Muse to… um, you."

My stomach dropped to my feet. "And then?"

Kane stepped up beside me, squeezing my hand in support.

Jade pressed her lips into a thin line. "I'm praying that you can neutralize it."

"And if I can't, I'll be the one in a coma? Are you sure we shouldn't wait for Bea?" Beatrice Kelton was the former New Orleans coven leader, a healer of sorts, and had a lot of knowledge. It wasn't that I didn't trust Jade. I did. But Bea had a lot more experience in this kind of thing.

"Believe me, I wish we could." Jade sighed and slumped against the wall as if she were exhausted. "But her energy is fading. I'm afraid if we don't do this now, we're going to lose her."

Crap.

We're doing it, Vienna said. Then my skin started to tingle and I got light-headed.

"Oh no you don't," I snapped. "Don't even think about taking over."

"Wha—?" Jade started, but I held my hand up, stopping her.

It was my magic that defeated Xavier, she said. *And I am the witch here. You probably have a better chance of survival if I'm the one who deals with it.*

"Are you talking to Vienna?" Kane asked.

I leaned into him, needing a safe place. "Yes. She wants to take over while we do this since it was technically her magic that defeated Xavier."

Jade tapped a finger against her lips. "It's not a bad idea."

Kane stiffened. "You want her to give herself over to the ghost?"

"Just while we work the spell." Jade had perked up and was already pulling candles out of her tote. "Now that I think about it, it's brilliant. Vienna and Muse are friends, have a connection. And Vienna is right. She knows how to wield magic. I think it's safer for everyone."

Kane ground his teeth together and tightened his jaw. "I don't like it. Maybe we should wait for Bea and the rest of the coven."

Jade stared pointedly at Muse. I followed her gaze. Muse's sunken cheeks and the dark circles under her eyes were haunting. She looked like death was knocking on her door.

We can't wait! Vienna shouted in my head, and suddenly I felt like my insides were going to explode. She was taking over, nearly pushing me out of my own body.

"Wait just a—" My voice was silenced and darkness washed over me. I blinked and refocused, once again seeing the world through Vienna's perspective. She had possession of my body and was staring down at Muse, tears rolling down my cheeks.

"I'm so sorry," she mumbled over and over again. "You didn't deserve this."

"Of course she didn't," Jade said in a soothing tone. "And neither did you."

Vienna turned, and I spotted Kane now standing a few feet from her, clutching his magical amulet. Interesting. He didn't trust her. That made me feel mildly better, but not much. If he blasted her, I'd actually be on the receiving end of his wrath. Still, knowing he was on guard was a small comfort.

Jade offered Vienna a white candle. The flame flickered from the slight sea breeze filtering in through the open sliding glass door. "The sooner we do this, the sooner you'll get to talk to her."

Vienna nodded. "What do you need me to do?"

Jade sat down next to Vienna on the bed and gently took Muse's hand in hers. Then she held her free hand out to Vienna. "I'm going to transfer the black magic from Muse to you. It's up to you to neutralize it."

Still clutching the candle, Vienna slipped my hand into Jade's. "Have you done this before?"

Jade nodded, her expression grave. "Yes."

I wanted to scream. Being relegated to the background when my body was being used for something so dangerous was a nightmare. But there wasn't anything to do about it. Even if I had a choice, I'd still volunteer to help Muse. Letting the woman fade away into the ether because of Xavier wasn't an option.

"I'm glad you agree," Vienna whispered under her breath, making it clear she was speaking to me.

Just make sure you save her and don't get us killed in the process, all right?

I'm already dead, remember? she shot back.

Double crap.

"Call up your magic," Jade told her.

Vienna nodded, and then her mind quieted. A faint electric current skittered through my veins, slower than it had before. It sputtered and stopped and started again. Vienna sucked in a deep breath of air, concentrating harder. Sweat beaded on my forehead, and my temple started to throb from the effort. This was not going well.

"Are you all right?" Jade asked, peering at her.

Vienna shook my head. "It's hard to access."

Jade nodded. "I was afraid of that. When we blasted the magic dragon, it took a real toll on Pyper and you as well. Most of your reserves were tied to it. Are you getting anything?"

"Yes. A bit, but it's like squeezing juice out of a dehydrated lemon."

Jade chuckled. "I can imagine. Here, let me see if I can help."

Vienna shrugged, and a moment later, I felt Jade's clear, clean energy rush through me. Suddenly my brain was on full alert and my normal energy level came roaring back. I bounced in the back of Vienna's mind, raring to go.

She shook her head, frustration making her scowl. "This isn't working. I can't—Oh." Something unlocked inside her, and magic rushed to her fingertips. She tilted her head and eyed

Jade. "How did you do that?"

She gave Vienna a serene smile. "I'm an empath. I sense your energy and emotions. All I did was tickle a bit of your reserves. But don't waste it. This small burst isn't going to last."

Vienna nodded. "Okay. Let's get on with it." She gazed down at Muse, concern eating away at her insides.

Jade started chanting something in Latin, and before I knew it, Vienna's energizing bolt of magic was gone, replaced by despair. Darkness closed in around me until I saw nothing but an empty blackness.

Vienna? The word sounded faint to my own ears.

A tremor ran through me and my bones chilled.

No answer.

Vienna! I tried again, but her name echoed in my mind.

She couldn't hear me. No one could. I imagined myself pounding desperately on a glass wall, trying to peer out into the void. Praying someone would notice me, let me out of my mental prison. No one responded. I shouted, only to hear my voice echo into the distance.

I tried to take deep breaths to calm myself, but I couldn't. I was suffocating, slipping away into a world of nothing where no one could hear me or see me. I was nothing but a fragment of a soul, trapped in darkness. In nothingness.

I was lost.

Everything ached. My frozen skin, my brittle bones, my raw throat. Even my eyes from the strain of trying to see in the darkness. Fatigue washed over me, and all I wanted to do was sleep. I drifted off, ready to be taken away. Ready to let the darkness swallow me. Warmth encircled me. Comfort. The pain was gone. Finally... I could sleep.

"Pyper!" Strong hands shook me.

I heard my name but couldn't open my eyes. My lids were too heavy. The ice was back.

A moan escaped from the back of my scratchy throat.

"Wake up, my love."

That voice. So rich, with just a lilt of an accent. So familiar. "Come on, baby. You can do it. Open your eyes." Something warm brushed over my cheek, soothing the icy chill.

"We need Bea," a woman said, her voice thick with tears. "I should've waited. What was I thinking?"

"You did what you thought was best," another male voice said. Another one I recognized but couldn't place. "She'll wake up. She has to."

Open your eyes, Pyper, the voice said in my head.

Go away.

Relief flooded through my heavy limbs. *There you are.*

I shook my head, or at least tried to, but wasn't certain I was able to move. All I wanted to do was go back to sleep.

"Pyper?" the tender male voice said again.

My heart ached to hear more of that voice. A small ball of warmth materialized in my chest and started a slow but steady pulse.

"She's in there. I can feel her." Jade's voice finally registered.

"Jade?" I croaked out and opened one eye. She was hovering over me, blocking the stream of sun coming in the window. She looked like a storybook angel sent from heaven with the light illuminating her.

She let out a gasp, and suddenly I was being smothered by my best friend's wife. "Thank the gods!"

"Jade," Kane said softly from behind her. "Let her breathe."

She laughed and let me go. Still hovering over me, she wiped at her eyes.

"Welcome back." Julius was sitting on my other side, staring down at me with a relieved smile.

"Hey." I lifted my hand and cupped his cheek. "I missed you."

He gave me a wry smile and lifted one eyebrow. "You sure do have a flair for the dramatic this trip."

I pushed myself up—again—and glanced around. "Did it work? Is Muse okay?"

Silence filled the room.

Son of a… "Where is she?"

Kane waved a hand, indicating the adjoining room. "She's in there. The spell didn't work. All it did was knock you out."

Jade covered her face with both hands, rubbing her forehead in frustration. "You were right. We should've waited for Bea."

"I want to see her," I said, already swinging my legs over the edge of the bed.

Julius put his hand on my arm. "You're sure you're okay?"

"Yes. I'm sure." That ball of pulsing energy in my chest was growing. It was feeding me, making it impossible to stay still.

"Okay." Julius hopped off the bed and opened the door for me.

Just inside, Muse was mirroring my recent position on the bed. Only she still looked like death.

Oh no, Vienna said. *I don't know what happened. One minute I was giving my magic to Jade and the next everything backfired. I was no longer in control and you were passed out.*

I could feel Vienna's desire to take over again, but I wasn't having it. That pulse of warm energy was enough to hold her back. "Jade? What was the spell supposed to do? Walk me through it."

She paled, then visibly swallowed. "I was supposed to take a thread of Vienna's magic, presumably magic that contains traces of Xavier's, and mix it with the black magic consuming Muse, then send it back to Vienna for her to neutralize. Only when I sent it back, all it did was knock you out. Nothing changed with Muse."

I sat down on the bed, studying the singer. The magic was still eating away at her. Jade hadn't gotten it all. She'd never wake up until she was free. It suddenly hit me that she was likely trapped in a dark place, just as I had been moments ago. What was it that brought me back? My friends' voices?

No. I heard them, but I didn't think that was it. It was something else. Something that I desperately didn't want to give up. The warm ball of energy pulsing in my chest. I didn't know what it was, or where it came from, but I knew Muse needed it.

"Jade?" I turned to her.

"Yes?"

"You need to try again. It'll work this time."

She shook her head. "No. I'll only hurt you."

"Maybe. Maybe not." The ball of energy grew and with it, I started to feel drawn to Muse. Like I had to help her. As if I didn't have a choice. "But this time is different." I grabbed her hand and pressed it to my chest. "Feel that?"

Her eyes widened. "Yes."

"It wasn't there before, was it?"

"No." Her voice took on a bit of awe. "It's powerful. Almost heady."

No kidding. It was making me feel invincible. Like I had a

purpose in life. "You need to use that. Give it to her. It'll break her out of her prison."

Jade dropped her hand. "I don't know…"

I stood, placing my hands on my hips. "I know. And I'm asking you to do this. Please, Jade."

She took a step back, shaking her head. "I can't."

"I will." Julius took her place beside me.

"This is not a good idea," Jade said, her voice rising in panic.

I stared up at him, my mouth parted in surprise. He just smiled down at me and squeezed my hand.

"Look at what happened last time," Jade said. "We can't just put them both in danger like that."

"I'm doing this. I have to," I said, softly. "There's magic inside me that can help her. I don't think I need it anymore." I turned to Julius. "Ready?"

"Ready." He reached for Muse's hand, and the second we were all joined, the ball of magic that had been pulsing in my chest shot down my arm and into Julius and straight into Muse.

I stumbled back, but Julius's grip kept me from toppling over, and while losing the energy ball didn't do me any favors, it hadn't knocked me out either. My legs were wobbly and a wave of fatigue hit me, making me long for a bed—the one in New Orleans with the overstuffed pillows and expensive sheets.

"Look," Jade whispered.

I blinked, clearing my vision, and stared at Muse. Her cheeks were flushed, her breathing more even, and her eyes were fluttering open.

The four of us stood there, no one saying a word, until finally Muse frowned and said, "Did I miss the party?"

Chapter 25

MUSE SAT ON my bed while I was busy packing my suitcase. After her ordeal, no one was comfortable with her being alone. Neither was she for that matter. Julius had disappeared to speak once again with the Witches' Council. Because we were still docked in Montego Bay, he was petitioning them to get us on the next flight back to New Orleans. We'd seen enough of the high seas. Jade and Kane had disappeared into their room to do their own packing.

"What are you going to do now?" I asked.

She plucked at the comforter. "I don't know. Concentrate on my music? Consider a solo career? I'm fairly certain the band is over me and my drama. It's probably better if I just go my own way."

I stuffed my lace-up boots in my suitcase. "If there is one thing I've learned these last few years, it's that friends, true friends, are family. Are you sure you want to cut them off without even trying to work it out?"

She shrugged. "It was never the same without Vienna."

The ghost in question, the one still taking up residence in my body, was eerily silent.

"It's stupid, you know. I was always jealous of her. Her

talent, her relationship, her fans. And then after… her accident, I sort of became a shell of her. Her band, her fans, her stalker. I guess in some twisted way, I sort of deserved what I got."

"No you didn't," I heard myself say. Only it wasn't my voice. It was Vienna's. I glanced down, once again noting her rings and the long blond, copper-streaked hair. She'd taken over, but I wasn't exactly just a spectator. I could've pushed her out but didn't see the need. Instead, I faded into the background, giving her and Muse their moment.

"Vienna?" Muse's eyes widened, then filled with tears. "It's true. You're here."

"I'm here." Vienna's words came out in a sob. "I'm here, Em. And oh, God, I'm so sorry. What happened with you with Xavier, you didn't deserve that. If I'd been stronger somehow, been able to reach someone, anyone, I could've saved you from that terrible fate."

"No!" Muse jumped off the bed and grabbed me by the shoulders. "Are you crazy? That bastard killed you, Vee. He threw you over the ship. What do you have to be sorry for?"

Vienna bit my lip and blinked back tears. "I saw what he was doing to you. I knew, but I couldn't figure out how to stop it. It wasn't until"—she waved at my body—"until Pyper came along and stood up to him that I was finally able to reach anyone. I just wish…" She shook my head. "I'd do anything to save you from these past years."

Muse let out a strangled, humorless laugh. "You have nothing to apologize for. I'm the one who knew Xavier was obsessed with you. If I'd warned someone, maybe this wouldn't have happened to either of us… or Razer. I'm not saying it's my fault. I'm done blaming anyone except that sicko creeper, but I can't stop thinking about how things could've been different… if I hadn't been so jealous. If I'd just said something—"

Vienna reached out and grabbed Muse, hugging her tightly. The other witch froze for just a second, then hugged her back. They both held on for a long time, the embrace soothing wounds that would likely never fully heal.

"I love you, Em," Vienna whispered. "It's not your fault. It never was. He had his hooks in me long before you ever knew anything about it. I should've confided in you."

"I love you too, Vee. And I'm sorry anyway. I miss you."

Vienna pulled back and studied the golden-haired witch. "Do me a favor?"

"Anything."

"Put everything you have into your music. Or anything else you're passionate about. Live for me. Love. Enjoy every moment you have, and never, ever, let anyone get in your way."

Geez. Her words made me want to cry. The passion radiating from her was inspiring.

Muse let out a choked sob and nodded. "I'll live for you. I'll make sure your music lives on."

"No. Make your own music. Let your voice be heard. If you want to play my songs, it's fine, but only do it if it's for you."

Muse smiled up at Vienna. "I like playing your songs. It makes me feel closer to you."

A single tear fell down my cheek, and I wasn't sure if Vienna was crying or if I was. These two loved each other like sisters. And I knew this was the last time they'd have this opportunity. I could sense Vienna's desire to move on.

"I'm going to miss you," Vienna said into her ear, and then just like that, she left my body and I morphed back into myself.

A weight lifted off me, and a heaviness that had settled in my chest was gone. I felt light and free and almost giddy. Until she'd left, I'd had no idea what a toll sharing my body had been.

Muse untangled herself from me and stepped back, wiping her eyes. "Sorry."

"No need to apologize." I gave her a reassuring smile, suddenly grateful I'd been able to be a conduit for them. "That must've been remarkable, seeing her after all this time."

Muse nodded. Then she moved toward the door. "I'm going to go have a word with the band, then I'll meet you all at the dock."

"Sure." I watched as she disappeared from the room. Hopefully she'd be able to find her footing now that her ordeal was over. I imagined therapy would be in order, but I hoped the next time we ran into her she'd be standing tall instead of falling-down drunk the way we'd found her just a few nights ago.

"She will be," Vienna said with confidence, still hovering near me.

"I hope so." I eyed her. "So your work here is done?"

She shrugged. "I guess so. I think it was my mission to make sure she was okay."

"And what about you?" I asked. "What will you do now?" The thought of her haunting the ship didn't sit well. Not after the hell she'd been put through. There had to be something we could do for her. I was just about ready to call on my guides for answers when she spoke again.

"I'm not sure, but I think there's somewhere I should be." She turned and moved toward the door.

"Want some company? Just in case?" After everything that

had happened, I felt weird about leaving her alone.

"Okay," she said as she slipped through the closed door.

After a hasty note to Julius to let him know where I was, I ran out the door. To my surprise, Vienna was waiting for me.

"I'm ready," I said.

She nodded and floated down the empty hallway.

✧   ✧   ✧

ROOM 1538 WAS eerily silent. No lights flickered. The temperature was stable. Flames didn't erupt in the mirrored wall. Nothing was out of place except the man standing in the middle of the room, staring just past my shoulder.

If I squinted, I could still see the outline of Julius in his dark suit, his tie undone, and thick dark hair, sticking out in spiky clumps.

But when I just gazed at him, all I saw was Razer. He was thin and lanky, had jet-black hair shoulder length, and was exactly what I'd expect from a typical rocker. He wore skintight, black leather plants, lace-up combat boots, and a T-shirt that read Sex, Drugs, and Black Magic Witches.

I smiled at that. It was a promo T-shirt from Vienna's band. Fan till the end.

"Razer," I heard the ghost behind me whisper, almost on a gasp.

His brilliant blue eyes bored into hers as he moved, his hand outstretched.

Vienna let out a strangled sob and ran to him. But when she got there, her ghostly body slid right through Julius's.

My heart nearly broke at the expression on both of their faces: devastation.

Razer was still using Julius's body, and solid for the moment, but Vienna wasn't. Not anymore. When she'd said goodbye to Muse, she'd been expelled from my body. I still didn't know why.

She hovered near him, wringing her hands.

He reached out to stop her but pulled back at the last minute and stuffed his hands in his pockets. "It's okay, love. We're here together, that's all that matters."

Tears welled in her beautiful eyes as she floated around him in a slow circle. "You don't understand."

"Of course I do." He moved with her, keeping his eyes locked on her lovely face. "I spent ten years in this room, waiting for you to come back to me. To hear your news. To make love to you before I gave you this." He pulled a small black-velvet box out of his pocket and lifted the lid.

A bright, shiny princess-cut diamond the size of a small boulder shone in the artificial light. Prisms bounced off the mirror and the ceiling.

Vienna's hand went to her open mouth, covering it as a fresh onslaught of tears streamed down her face. "You were…" She gasped in a small sob. "It was true."

He took a tiny step closer to her, still holding the ring out. "What's true, Vivi?"

She let out a choked laugh as she closed her eyes. "Muse told me you were going to propose." Vienna reached out, and even though she couldn't hold on to him with her ghost body, she lined her palm up with his heart and held it there. "I can feel your strong heartbeat."

Razer shook his head sadly. "No, that's Julius's. He kindly let me share his body while we investigated what happened to you. I'm afraid my heart stopped beating the moment I learned you were lost as sea."

She shook her head. "You're still in there. I can feel you."

Razer lifted his arms to simulate wrapping them around her.

She let out a sigh and tilted her head to the side as if were resting it on his chest.

And as I stood there watching their tragedy play out, something broke inside me. A dam of built-up emotions burst, and without thinking, I moved toward them. There was nothing to consider. All I felt was their love. It was all around me, pressing in on me, propelling me forward. They'd suffered enough. We'd shared my body before; we could do it again. I had something I could give her, and I'd never forgive myself if I didn't.

"Lily?" I whispered to myself.

My guide materialized beside me, a proud expression claiming her soft features. *Are you ready?*

"I am."

Razer's eyes opened, then widened as he spotted me standing right behind the shadowy form of Vienna. "What are you doing?"

I held up a hand and gave him a genuine smile. "My gift to you both." Then I glanced at Lily. "Now."

My guide beamed at me as she waved a hand. My other guide, Tru, appeared. "Good evening, Pyper. I see you're embracing your new ability."

I nodded. "I just need a little help."

Tru nodded to Lily and the pair of them stood behind me, side by side, shoulder to shoulder.

"All you need to do is open your mind and your heart," Lily

whispered into my ear.

I continued to stare at Razer as I nodded.

"Now, find the connection. If you can ground yourself to the Earth somehow, you can share your body like a shell without being compromised," Lily said.

It was funny that I was doing this on a ship and not solid ground. Jade would've killed me if she knew I was willingly inviting Vienna back into my being. No doubt she'd have had me wait until we got back to New Orleans so she could call on the coven and insist we use the coven circle.

But I knew better. There was one thing—one person, really—that kept me tethered in place.

Julius.

And he was standing right in front of me. At the thought of him, Razer's form faded to Julius's. His bright green eyes sparkled at me as he gave me a short nod of approval.

"I'm here, Pyper," he said, his voice now his own, soft and reassuring. "I won't let you go."

I knew he wouldn't. I could open myself up to every spirit on the high seas, and he'd still be there, anchoring me to him. "Ready?" I asked him.

He nodded and reached for my hand.

A current of electricity zinged up my arm when our fingers brushed. Immediately upon contact, Razer was back, that confused expression still plaguing his face. I just smiled, knowing what was to come.

"Release your barriers," Tru instructed. "Imagine your invisible walls being torn down one by one".

I did as she asked. My imaginary fortress of entwined jasmine vines slowly unraveled. I envisioned sunshine beaming down on me, exposing me to the outside world.

"Now invite her in," Tru added.

"Vienna?" I whispered, barely recognizing my own voice. Everything was raw, my defenses stripped away. I'd never felt so vulnerable and powerful at the same time. I had something important to give. Something that was bigger than me or Julius.

Love.

The word floated around in my mind, grew, and sent warmth straight to my toes. I'd never felt so satisfied, so needed, so selfless.

A cool, soothing balm settled over my soul, and suddenly I had the feeling I was no longer in my body… or rather, was no longer in control of it.

"Pyper?" The familiar voice echoed in my mind, and when I turned, I spotted Julius lounging on an overstuffed white love seat, his arm resting along the back as he stared down past me.

I followed his gaze and grinned. Vienna was wrapped in Razer's arms, the pair of them holding each other for dear life.

"Sit with me," Julius said, waving me over.

I glanced down, noting we were in some sort of loft area, overlooking the rocker couple before us. It had to be an illusion. But it didn't bother me. Everything about the moment was perfect.

I smiled at Julius and sort of floated over to him, but when I sat, the cushions gave way to my weight and the arm Julius put around me was just as solid as it always was.

"You did a good thing," he said into my ear, nuzzling my neck.

"I think so too." I slid my hand over to his free one, entwining my fingers in his. "Is this what it's been like for you the entire time you've been sharing your body with Razer?"

He chuckled. "No. Not even close. The light didn't come on until Vienna stepped into your body."

I studied him. "Explain."

He waved a hand, indicating the entire room. "Before you let Vienna in, when Razer was in charge, it was more like I was sitting in a dark corner of my own mind, watching everything, hearing what he had to say but unable to participate until his energy waned. But then as soon as you gave Vienna permission to utilize your body, it was like a light switch came on and I was able to leave the confines of my mind to enjoy a little distance from him. It's a bonus that you're here too."

I chuckled and shook my head. "That is exactly what it was like when Vienna forced her way into my body. But this, inviting her? It changed everything."

There was a tug in my belly, a solid connection to Vienna and the body she used, but no real need to get back anytime soon. It was very different than when I'd been carrying a second soul. I was still me, my soul completely my own, and I knew I was still in charge. The moment I asked Vienna to leave, she would. There was no danger of soul fusing here, at least not for me. I felt it in my bones.

"How are you feeling?" I asked him.

"Fine. Like I'm me again. The hold Razer had on me has lifted. I could cast him out at any second." He gazed down at the pair now. They had their heads bent together, whispering in confidence. "But I'm not in any hurry." Turning his attention to me once again, he added, "Especially since you're here."

I leaned into him, resting my head on his shoulder as I gazed up at him. "You're right. We did a good thing here."

Julius's eyes softened, and then he tilted his head and gently brushed a kiss over my lips. As he pulled away, he traced his thumb over my cheek, the tenderness in his touch making my heart swell. "You're really something special, you know that?"

"No more special than you are."

Raising one eyebrow, he gave me a skeptical look. "I'd argue that what you did here today goes well beyond selflessness. There were any number of times over the past few days where I would've gladly ejected Razer from my being. And to be honest, even though I wouldn't change this outcome, I still resent knowing he was a part of me, that he was onboard when we almost…" He cleared his throat. "Well, you know what I mean. Your heart is about ten times bigger than the average human."

I didn't know what to say to any of that, so I wrapped my free arm around him and held on, enjoying the steady beat of his heart in my ear.

"Pyper?" His arms tightened around me.

"Yeah?"

He gently lifted me away from him just enough so that he could look me in the eye. "I'm going to kiss you now."

My lips twitched with a small smile. After a moment, I said, "I'm waiting."

His gaze shifted to my mouth, and I rewarded him by wetting my lips with the tip of my tongue.

He pulled me onto his lap so that I was straddling him, tilted his head, and then kissed me. Kissed me like a starving man. And I responded in kind, unleashing all my pent-up frustration, branding him with my kiss, making sure he knew exactly what I wanted from him.

The world around us fell away. I knew nothing but Julius's

heated touch, his gentle but demanding grip, and his faint rosewood scent. I could've stayed locked in his embrace forever, drinking in his kisses. But all too soon he pulled away, both of us breathless.

"I wasn't done," I said, pressing a soft kiss to the corner of his mouth.

His hand tightened on my thigh as he smiled at me and nodded toward the door. "But they are."

I twisted, realizing for the first time we weren't in some loft overlooking Razer and Vienna. We were on the small couch of the stateroom, and the pair was moving toward the door hand in hand, their bodies translucent.

I glanced down at our joined bodies. "They left us already."

He nodded. "Looks like they're both free now."

I swallowed the lump forming in my throat and watched as the pair turned and waved at us.

A twinge of regret mixed with pride filled me. I raised my hand and waved good-bye just as the pair shimmered brightly with silver light and then faded into the ether.

"They're gone, aren't they?" I asked Julius, surprised at the hint of sadness mingling with my relief.

He nodded. "Yes. And at peace, finally."

"Together," I added.

"Just the way it should be." He clutched my hand and stood. "Let's go. There's a bottle of champagne and a tray of gourmet cheeses waiting for us on a private plane."

A slow smile spread across my face. "Champagne?"

He chuckled. "You didn't think I was going to let the council off too easily did you? Come on. I'm more than ready to leave this boat behind."

I stood, curling my fingers around his. "Just one more stop."

He raised an eyebrow.

"There's a ghost waiting for me at the Green Parrot."

Chapter 26

THE GREEN PARROT was empty save one lone customer sitting at the bar.

Muse.

"Hey," I said, taking the seat next to her, noting her luggage piled up at her feet. Julius had left me to my task and was busy taking care of our own suitcases. "I thought we were meeting you on the dock."

"It turns out someone needed my help with something." She gave me a small smile and inclined her head toward a table a few feet away.

Bootlegger was sitting in a booth, in solid form, nursing a shot of whiskey.

I raised my eyebrows in surprise. "That's new."

"It's temporary. He said he has to make amends but didn't know how. I figured after everything you all did for me, I could pay it forward."

"That's... kind of you. But where's Cal and his girlfriend?" Without the couple in question, Bootlegger wasn't going to be able to make good on his promise to Madeline.

"We found Cal. He was sulking in his stateroom. The girl-friend was down at the beach, but he was able to reach her. The only way he could convince her to come back before the ship is ready to depart was to promise her some time with me." Her face flushed bright pink. "I haven't interacted with a fan sober in… I don't know how long."

I glanced at the ice water in front of her and gave her a nod of approval. "You'll do fine."

"I hope so."

"Just what the fresh hell is going on here?" I heard Ida May cry from across the room.

Muse and I both turned to find her hovering over Bootlegger.

He glanced up at her but said nothing. Instead, he raised his shot of whiskey in a salute and downed it.

Ida May turned and pressed her hands to her hips, her face scrunched up like a petulant child's. "Why is he solid and I'm not?"

Muse nodded toward the bar entrance. The door had just opened and Cal was holding it open for his girlfriend.

Ida May flew over to us. "What do they have to do with anything?"

"Bootlegger is making amends," I said as Muse got up to greet them.

The woman's face was flushed with excitement while they took pictures and Muse signed autographs.

"With the guy he possessed the other night?" Ida May's anger dissipated as she processed the information.

"Yep," I said and signaled to the bartender. "Another water, please?"

Ida May rolled her eyes. "You are such a square."

I nodded. Today I was anyway. Before long, I watched as

Muse led Cal and his girlfriend over to Bootlegger. The old pirate got to his feet, shook their hands, then bowed his head as he tried to explain the situation.

"Oh, this is good," Ida May said, chuckling.

I had to agree. The skepticism on the girlfriend's face was classic. But then Muse reached out and touched Bootlegger, turning him transparent.

"Where did he go?" she cried.

Once again Muse reached out, but this time she touched the girlfriend.

Her eyes went wide in shock. "He's transparent!"

"Duh," Ida May said. She turned to me. "I'm bored."

"Don't worry. We're leaving soon. I'm sure there's some trouble you can get up to in New Orleans."

She tsked. "I was hoping to get up to Bootlegger later."

"I doubt that's going to happen." I tilted my head toward the end of the bar. Madeline had appeared and was standing primly, her hands clasped as she waited for Bootlegger to finish apologizing.

"Who is that?"

Madeline turned and waved to us, a pleasant smile on her face.

"Bootlegger's significant other. I imagine as soon as he's done, they'll be reuniting."

"Reuniting!" she all but shouted. "That two-timing, no good pirate. This vacation sucks."

"It was never a vacation. We were here to—"

"Oh, forget it." She glared at Madeline, then Bootlegger, then me.

I just smiled at her. "Sorry."

Her lips formed a thin line, and I swore I saw smoke come out of her ears. "What's a ghost gotta do in order to get a little sexy time? For the love of—" She let out a heavy sigh, glanced once at Bootlegger, then back at me. "This ship sucks. See you at the Grind."

There was a small pop as she vanished into thin air.

Madeline glanced over at me, her eyebrows raised in question.

I shook my head, then smiled as I noticed Cal and his girl-friend leaving the bar. He had his arm around her, kissing the top of her head as she leaned into him, holding on as if she'd never let go.

"That worked out," Muse said, striding up to me. She grabbed her luggage. "Ready?"

I nodded and waved to Bootlegger and Madeline as they too drifted off hand in hand.

What was that? Three for three reunions in the past few hours?

Grinning, I dropped a tip on the bar and stood. "Ready."

✧   ✧   ✧

THE FLIGHT HOME had been luxurious if not eventful. Julius and I, Kane and Jade, and Muse shared the small private plane, landing at Louis Armstrong International just after midnight. The council had taken Xavier into custody. The ship had declared the paranormal activity resolved, and four ghosts had been set free. Not bad for three days' worth of work, if I did say so myself.

"I can't wait to get some sleep," Julius said, holding my apartment door open.

I walked in, flipped the light on, and nearly wept in relief. Home.

The place smelled faintly of freshly ground coffee and was so welcoming I contemplated collapsing right there on my overstuffed couch. Instead, I dropped my luggage and headed for the floor-to-ceiling windows and stared out over Bourbon Street, smiling at the familiar sights of tourists milling around below.

Julius walked up behind me and wrapped his arms around my waist. "Good to be home?"

I nodded and leaned into him. "Tell me you're not going to sleep in your room tonight."

He sucked in a small breath. Julius was technically my roommate. Not long after he'd transitioned from ghost status to human status, I'd offered him a room. Since then he'd been on his best behavior, insisting he sleep there until our relationship reached that crucial level. The one that meant we were headed toward something permanent. Something that meant rings and commitment. He was sort of old-fashioned. Heck, not sort of. He *was* old-fashioned, and the idea of living together wasn't exactly in his comfort zone.

"You know how I feel about this. Moving too fast—"

I turned around and met his gaze head-on. "We slept in the same bed on the ship."

"That's not quite the same."

"No. It's not. And I understand why you wanted to keep separate bedrooms. Not move too fast. I really do. But here's where I'm coming from—after this week's ordeal, all I want is to feel safe in your arms. I want to know that if I wake up in the middle of the night, you'll be there."

He was quiet for a moment, then he leaned in and gently kissed me. "I think that sounds reasonable."

"Reasonable?" I chuckled. "Who says that?"

He smiled down at me. "Men who are honorable."

"Men who are infuriating." I smiled back at him. "Come on. It's late."

"Just as long as you don't plan to take advantage of me, Ms. Rayne. You know I have standards." He winked and slid his fingers between mine.

"Right. You and your standards. But don't worry, tonight I just want to sleep. Tomorrow you can worry about your virtue."

He laughed and tugged me into the bedroom.

After we each performed our nightly routines, I climbed into bed wearing a tank top and night shorts. Julius was in sleep shorts, his glorious chest bare, lying on his back with his hands clasped behind his head.

I rolled over and cuddled up next to him.

"Is this your normal nightly attire?" he asked, glancing down at me.

"Nope." I gave him my flirty smile. "But I didn't want to offend your wholesome honor."

A flash of heat flickered through his eyes, but when he blinked it was gone. "I appreciate it."

I let out a huff of laughter. "Right."

He tightened his hold on me, pulling me closer, and kissed the top of my head. "Good night, love."

"Good night, Julius."

As I lay there listening to his breathing turn steady, I gazed at our entwined legs, illuminated by the sliver of moonlight shining through the gap in the drapes. Peace washed over me, and for the first time in weeks, I felt like I was exactly where I was supposed to be. In Julius's arms.

I lifted my head and placed a soft kiss to his lips and whispered, "I think I love you."

He made a small contented sound and mumbled something unintelligible in his sleep.

Smiling, I tucked my head against his shoulder and instantly fell into a deep sleep.

✧   ✧   ✧

I WOKE IN the dead of the night, reaching for Julius. But all I found was an empty bed. I sat up, rubbing at my eyes, and spotted him standing at the window just as I had when we'd returned home a few hours ago. "Hey," I said, my voice heavy with sleep. "What's going on."

He turned, a gentle smile on his face. "Sorry. I didn't mean to wake you."

"You didn't." I threw the covers off and swung my legs over the side of the bed. By the time I was on my feet, he was already by my side.

"Hey, there's no need to get up." He brushed the hair out of my eyes, letting his hand trail down my neck, making a delicious shiver tingle down my spine.

I stared into his heated gaze and on impulse licked my lips.

His eyes flickered to my mouth, lingering there.

My entire body seemed to flush, and I had to stop myself from swaying into him. I cleared my throat. "Is it me? Am I the one keeping you up? I guess sharing a bed wasn't such a good—"

"Shh." He cut me off as his free hand cupped my hip, pulling me forward.

I raised my eyebrows. "I thought we were just going to sleep."

"We were." He buried his hand in my hair and pulled me closer. "That was before you told me you think you love me."

My breath caught and words failed me as my mouth worked.

His beautiful eyes flashed with pleasure as he lowered his mouth to mine and kissed me, an all-consuming kiss that left me dazed and weak-kneed.

When he finally pulled back, he cupped both of my cheeks and said, "I think I love you too, my wild girl. There's nowhere else I want to be and no one else I want to be with."

My heart nearly exploded. And instead of answering, I climbed back into the bed, tugging him along with me. He followed without resistance, lying on his side while I leaned back against the pillows.

"You're gorgeous," he said, resting his hand on my stomach.

"And you're exactly what I need." I pulled him down, and this time when we kissed, there weren't any barriers. No hesitations. Only us, our passion, and more love than I'd ever thought possible.

Afterward, as I lay in his arms, safe and satisfied, my heart swelled and happy tears stung my eyes. "Julius?" I whispered.

"Yeah, love?"

"I don't think I've ever been this happy."

He was silent for a moment, tracing his fingertips over my bare arm. Then he kissed my neck, slowly working his way up to my mouth. But before he pressed his lips to mine, he met my gaze and said, "I'm certain I've never been this happy."

A grin tugged at my lips.

"Just like I'm certain I love you."

"Julius," I breathed.

"And that I'm going to love you forever."

Happiness like I'd never known exploded through me. And unable to speak, I rolled so I was on top of him and proceeded to show him just exactly what he meant to me.

Chapter 27

"THIS PLACE IS a tomb," Ida May complained.

"So go somewhere else," I said as I poured the soy milk into Jade's iced chai tea latte.

Jade walked in from the back, glancing at me and then at the handwritten chalkboard. She laughed and read Ida May's contribution out loud. "Bitter Beans and Franks? What is that?"

I pulled a tray out of the pastry case and passed her the chopped-up éclair that was sitting on a bed of whole coffee beans. "Ida May said the éclair had it coming."

"It did. All it does is sit there, taunting me." She flew around the Grind in a whirlwind of frustrated energy.

Jade started when Ida May knocked a row of spices over, causing them to crash to the floor. "I see she's still a little upset."

"Just a bit," I agreed, not sure what to do for a disgruntled ghost.

We'd been back from the ill-fated cruise for over a week and a day hadn't gone by when Ida May hadn't been grumpy. Her thwarted tryst with Bootlegger had left her… well, frustrated.

"Just because you're getting it on with the live-in boyfriend doesn't mean you have to be so danged chipper all the time."

I chose to ignore her last remark and handed Jade her drink.

"Thanks." She took a sip and then peered at me. "I thought you were taking the day off?"

"I was, but Holly called in hungover, so I opened for her."

Jade shook her head, glancing at the clock. She pulled her phone out of her pocket, tapped out a text, then smiled a moment later when she got a reply. "Charlie will be here within the hour."

I gave her a flat stare. "That wasn't necessary."

"Yes it was. You've worked every single day since we got back. I know you love the café, but goodness, woman, it's time to go enjoy that boyfriend of yours." She waved a hand toward the front of the shop.

Just then I heard and more importantly felt the loud rumble of a motorcycle.

"Now we're talking," Ida May said and flew through the glass front door, causing the bell to chime.

I leaned against the counter, waiting to see what Ida May was going to do.

"Pyper," Jade said. "Aren't you going to go out there?"

"Why?" Plate glass windows lined the front of my shop, giving me a clear view. "I can see perfectly well from here. Well, as long as she doesn't stray too far."

"She?" Jade's pale brow furrowed. "Oh, you mean Ida May?" She laughed. "No, silly. Check out the hottie sitting on that motorcycle."

I turned and peered out the window once more. Then I felt it, the stupid happy grin that claimed my face every time I saw him.

Julius.

He was sitting on the cruiser, holding his helmet while Ida

May spun around in circles, her hands waving wildly. I chuckled. "Looks like Ida May finally found something to pull her out of her funk."

"Let me guess? The motorcycle?" Jade asked.

I nodded, still grinning stupidly at my man. Damn, he looked good on a Harley.

"Of course she would be excited about that." Jade rolled her eyes. "That ghost would be happy to sit on a washing machine on spin cycle."

I started at her words and then burst out laughing. But only because it was true. Ida May was... let's just say a little preoccupied with the opposite sex these days. "Funny," I said, through my chortles.

Jade snorted out a laugh and waved her hand toward the street again. "Go on. I've got this place under control."

I shook my head. "Not hard when it's a ghost town," I said, stating the obvious. But we both knew that at a half past eleven, there'd likely be a line out the door. It was why she'd called Charlie.

"Get out. Go have fun. Don't come back for a few days." She started organizing the pastry case, consolidating and making room for fresh items.

"I'll be back tonight," I said, moving toward the door.

"That's what you think," she said.

I paused with my hand on the door handle. "What?"

She smiled brightly at me. "Nothing. Go on. Have a good time. Everything's covered here."

I frowned, studying her. "You're being kind of weirder than normal. Are you all right?"

She let out a huff of mock irritation. "I'm *fine*. Go. Julius is waiting."

"All right, I'm going. Thanks for covering for me."

She waved and went back to restocking for the lunch rush.

I pulled my apron off, tossed it on a table, and strode out into the glorious sunshine. Julius was sitting on that mighty bike, grinning at me.

"Ready for a ride?" he asked, holding up a second helmet.

"Where did you get that thing? And do you even know how to work it?" Considering he'd been alive in the early nineteen hundreds and only lived in the twenty-first century for a short time, it wasn't like he'd had ample opportunity to take riding lessons.

"As a matter of fact, I do know how to work it. It's got a little more power than the one I had in twenty-two, but I think I can manage."

Nineteen twenty-two. Almost one hundred years ago. The realization should've boggled my mind. Made me stop and pause. Instead, I just grinned at him like an idiot.

"Pyper! Have you seen this baby?" Ida May asked, running a hand over the back fender as if it were a lover.

"Yes, Ida, I see it."

Julius glanced behind him, then back at me with his lips pressed together. "Are we going to have company on our ride?"

"You bet your butt—" Ida May started, then froze. She was hovering in the middle of Bourbon Street, a frown tugging at her lips. "Something's wrong. I—Oh my word. I've never had that happen before." Her eyes met mine, round and full of surprise. Then she let out a small yelp and vanished from her spot with a loud poof.

Julius jumped, nearly losing his footing while holding up the bike. "What the hell just happened?"

I shrugged, not really concerned. That wasn't the first time Ida May had just disappeared on me. I was certain it wouldn't be the last. I held out a hand, taking Julius's extra helmet.

He handed it to me, then patted the saddlebags. "Ready for a road trip?"

I eyed the saddlebag, wondering what he'd packed. "How long?"

He shrugged. "Does it matter?"

I didn't move as I glanced back and forth between the bike and the Grind. "It does if I have to worry about staffing the café."

His smile widened. "Jade has that covered for us. Right now all that's important is that we have some fun. Where do you want to go?" The bike started to rumble beneath him, and any hesitations I might've had flew right out the window.

This was Julius on a Harley. What was I waiting for?

Still holding my helmet, I threw one leg over the back of the bike and then settled in behind him.

Julius twisted, caught my lips with one of his signature searing kisses, then asked, "Well? Do you have a preference on what you'd like to see?"

I shook my head. "Anything. River Road, the Bayou, Grand Isle? Anywhere you want to take me."

His smile turned seductive. "Believe me, I'm taking you to new places later tonight. Right now I'm thinking a cruise in the bayou."

"Sounds perfect."

He revved the throttle on the bike, making it rumble beneath us. And on that note, I pulled my helmet on, wrapped my arms around him, and held on for the ride of my life.

Deanna's Book list:

Pyper Rayne Novels
Spirits, Stilettos, and a Silver Bustier
Spirits, Rock Stars, and a Midnight Chocolate Bar
Spirits, Beignets, and a Bayou Biker Gang

Jade Calhoun Novels
Haunted on Bourbon Street
Witched of Bourbon Street
Demons of Bourbon Street
Angels of Bourbon Street
Shadows of Bourbon Street
Incubus of Bourbon Street
Bewitched on Bourbon Street

Crescent City Fae Novels
Influential Magic
Irresistible Magic
Intoxicating Magic

Destiny Novels
Defining Destiny
Accepting Fate

About Deanna

New York Times and USA Today bestselling author, Deanna Chase, is a native Californian, transplanted to the slower paced lifestyle of southeastern Louisiana. When she isn't writing, she is often goofing off with her husband in New Orleans, playing with her two shih tzu dogs, or making glass beads. For more information and updates on newest releases visit her website at deannachase.com.

Made in the USA
San Bernardino, CA
23 July 2017